Trading Jeff and his Dog

Jim Kjelgaard

Must Have Books
503 Deerfield Place
Victoria, BC
V9B 6G5
Canada
trava2911@gmail.com

ISBN: 9781773236254

Copyright 2019 – Must Have Books

For
Margaret Mary, John, Jim, Frank, and Barbara Dresen

I. THE MEETING

When the dog came to the weed-grown border of the clearing, he stopped. Then, knowing that his back could be seen over the weeds, he slunk down so that his belly scraped the earth. He was tense and quivering, and his eyes bore a haunted look. But there was nothing craven in them and little fear. In all his life the dog had never feared anything except the terrible torment that beset him now.

He was of no recognizable breed, though all of his ancestors had been large dogs. There was a hint of staghound in his massive head and in his carriage, and somewhere along the way he had acquired a trace of Great Dane. His fur was silky, like a collie's, and there was a suggestion of bloodhound in his somewhat flabby jowls. Without purpose or plan, the blood of all these breeds had mingled to produce this big mongrel.

He was so emaciated that slatted ribs showed even through his burr- matted fur. Had he eaten as much as he wanted, he would have weighed about a hundred and ten pounds, but he had had so little food recently that he was fifteen pounds lighter. Intelligence glowed in his eyes. But there was also something in them that verged on desperation.

He moved only his head and moved that slowly. This dog knew too much, and had suffered too much, to let himself be seen until he had some idea of what he was about. He was looking toward a big white farmhouse that was surrounded by a grove of apple trees. A thin plume of blue smoke rose from the chimney, and a pile of freshly-split wood lay in the yard. Busy white hens wandered about. White and black cows and two brown horses cropped grass in a pasture. Pigs grunted in their pen and a black cat sunned itself on the door step.

The dog's attention returned to the man who was splitting more wood. He was thin, dressed in faded blue jeans and a tan shirt, and the blows of his axe echoed dully from the hills surrounding the farm house. He worked slowly and methodically. The dog drank eagerly of his scent, although he did not leave his cover, for behind

3

him there was only a trail of torment, abuse and real danger. He had been wandering for two months and his path was a long one, but because it was also a twisted one it had not taken him too far from the place he had left. He had been in villages and towns, through farm lands and forest, and wherever he met men he had been stoned or clubbed. Three times-twice by farmers and once by a policeman-he had been shot at.

The dog could not know that this was partly because of his appearance and size. He was big and he looked wild. Had he cared to do so, he could have killed a man. But what none of his tormentors could know was that, though the dog feared little, he was almost incapable of attacking a human being. What nobody could know either was that, most of all, the dog was in desperate need of someone to love.

Until two months ago, everything had been different. When the dog came to live with Johnny Blazer, in the hills behind Smithville, he was so young that it always seemed he must have begun life with Johnny. It was a good life and he had never wanted any other.

Johnny's cabin was big, with a kitchen and combined living-dining room on the first floor and the entire second floor given over to many bunks. It was necessary to have a big cabin because, in season, Johnny both guided and boarded hunters and fishermen. During the winter, he trapped furs, and when there was nothing else to do he worked at odd jobs or searched out and sold medicinal roots which he found in the hills. A lean, tight-jawed woodsman in his late thirties, Johnny had been the dog's revered master.

Because he was a dog, and thus incapable of grasping the more complex facts, the great animal did not understand that life was not the wholly carefree and happy one it seemed. He could sense that Johnny avoided the Whitneys, who-at various places in the hills-lived much as Johnny did. Because they were Johnny's enemies, it followed that the Whitneys must be the dog's enemies too. But he had never understood what took place.

Johnny and the dog were strolling toward Smithville when a rifle cracked and Johnny took three staggering steps to fall forward. While the dog hovered anxiously near, his master tried and failed to get up. The dog knew that the scent of Pete Whitney filled the air, but there was no connection between Pete and the fact that Johnny Blazer lay wounded in the road.

For an hour the dog worried beside Johnny, whining because he could not help. Then a car happened along. The two men in it lifted Johnny into the car and were off at high speed.

The dog tried to follow, but though he could run very fast, he could not keep up with the car. Outdistanced, he panted back to the cabin because he was sure that Johnny would return there, too. He waited a week, never venturing far away and eating only what he could find or catch. Then he set out to look for Johnny.

He'd gone first to Smithville and the first person he'd met there was Pete Whitney. The dog slowed to a walk, watching Pete warily and bristling. He saw no connection between any of Pete's actions and Johnny's disappearance, but all the Whitneys were enemies. He leaped aside when Pete aimed a swift kick at his groin,

4

then turned with bared fangs. Unarmed, Pete shrank back against a near-by building and the dog went on.

The alarm was sounded; Johnny Blazer's dog had come into town and threatened a person. For a while-Johnny had many friends in Smithville- nothing was done. But after two days, the dog was considered a menace. Mothers of small children became concerned for their safety. The first act of most men, upon seeing the dog, was to pick up and hurl any convenient missile.

The Smithville constable, Bill Ellis, reluctantly set out to kill the animal. But two hours earlier, having satisfied himself that he would not find Johnny in Smithville, the dog had left. What he could not possibly know was that his master was dead and the official cause of his death was, "Bullet wound inflicted by a person or persons unknown."

As the dog wandered, hope faded. He could not find Johnny. But the dog had to have a master because he was unable to live without one, and now, as he lay in the tall weeds, all the deep yearnings in his heart concentrated on this man splitting wood.

He half rose, minded to walk out and meet him, but memory of the rocks and clubs that had come his way was not an easy one to banish and he settled down in the weeds again. Then an uncontrollable longing for someone to love and someone to love him overcame everything else and he left the weeds.

He walked with his tail drooping in a half circle down his rear, but he was not abject because it was not in him to be so. One or more of his many ancestors had bequeathed to him a great pride and a regal inner sense, and though he would run when a club or brick was hurled at him, he could never cringe. He carried his tail low because that was the way he carried it naturally, like a collie or staghound.

The man, setting a chunk of wood against the splitting block, had his back turned to the dog and did not at once see him. The dog waited, unwilling to intrude until he was invited to do so. The man raised his axe, brought it expertly down, and the wood split cleanly. He stooped to pick up the two pieces and when he did he saw the dog.

"You!"

Catching up one of the chunks, he hurled it with deadly aim and intent. But even as he did this, the huge animal started to run, so that instead of striking him in the head, the chunk of wood struck his right shoulder. The dog felt quick agony that subsided to searing pain as he kept running. Twenty seconds later he heard a rifle blast, and the thump of a leaden slug that plowed into the earth six inches to one side. The rifle roared a second time, and a third. Then he was safe in the woods.

He slowed to a walk, knowing that he could not be seen now and his nose informed him that there were no other men around. For the time being he was in no danger, but he was heartsick. Again he had tried, in every way he

knew, to find someone whom he might love and who in turn might love him. Once more his overtures had brought him only hurt.

The dog could not know that the farmer, seeing him suddenly, had been too startled to think. When he was finally capable of coherent thought, he decided that a wild, dangerous and doubtless rabid wolf had emerged from the forest and that its

5

only intention could be to prey upon the locality's flocks and herds. Failing to bring it down with his rifle, the farmer got hastily on the phone to mobilize his neighbors. Within half an hour a posse was out.

However, its members were farmers and not hunters. The only hunting dogs in the area were a few fox and coon hounds and some rabbit hounds, and they refused to interest themselves in the supposed wolf's trail. But there was also a pair of big cross-bred brindle bulls and they were urged into the woods. An hour later the dog met this pair.

Coursing a little open glade, they appeared in front of him and as soon as they saw him they stopped. The bulls weighed only about fifty pounds each, but they had had many battles and they knew how to fight. Lifting their lips in anticipatory grins, they closed in.

The dog waited, anger rising in his heart. He too knew how to fight. For the barest fraction of a minute he gauged the bulls' advance, then he attacked. He was not as swift as he ordinarily was because he had not eaten enough. But with his staghound and collie lineage, he had inherited all the fluid, rippling grace of such dogs. It was not his way to bore in, to seek a hold and keep it, but to slash and slice. He struck the first bull, cut it to the shoulder bone, and leaped clear over his enemy before there could be a return thrust. He whirled to face the second.

It came at him with a short, choppy gait, eyes half closed and mouth open as it sought any hold at all. As soon as it was able to get one, it would clamp its jaws and grind until the piece of flesh in its mouth was torn out. Then it would get another hold, and another, and literally tear its enemy apart.

The dog waited, as though he were about to meet the bull head on. But when only inches separated them, he glided to one side, ducked to get hold of a front leg, and used all his strength to throw the bull clear over his head. He turned to meet the second bull that, recovering, had come in to grab his thigh.

Twisting himself almost double, the dog slashed and bit and each time he slashed fresh blood spurted from the brindle bull's hide. The dog opened his huge mouth, clamped it over the bull's neck, and shook his adversary back and forth.

The bulls had courage, but they were cross-breeds and not the fighting bulls that will gladly die if they can take their enemy with them. They staggered twenty feet off and faced the dog warily, as though seeking some new way to attack him. He waited, ready for whatever they might do, and when he finally limped away he did so with his head turned to see if he was being followed.

He was not afraid to renew the battle, but he wanted most to be let alone by this ugly pair. In spite of all the rebuffs and even physical violence that he had met up with, however, he could not abandon the driving urge that had sent him forth. He could not live without a master. Somewhere and somehow he must find one.

He passed from settled country into forest where there was only an occasional clearing. When two deer fled before him he gave halfhearted chase. But his shoulder still hurt and the battle had wearied him. When the deer outdistanced him, he stopped to eat a few mushrooms that grew on a stump. They were tasteless fare, but they helped still the gnawing in his belly. Near the edge of a pond, he found and ate a fish

6

that had been hurt in battle with a bigger fish, and after that he caught a mouse. All together were mere tidbits, and the dog thought wistfully of the delicious meals Johnny Blazer used to prepare for him.

Night had fallen when he stopped suddenly, his nose tickled by the tantalizing odor of food. Mingled with it was the smell of wood smoke and a man. The dog's nose informed him that there was a creek, and he caught the faintly-acrid smell of cinders and steel that meant a railroad. The dog slowed to a walk and went closer to verify with his eyes what his nose had already told him.

There was a creek spanned by a railroad bridge. Beneath the bridge was a small, bright fire over which, on a forked stick, hung a pot of simmering coffee. Crouched beside the fire was a man, and because there is a difference in the odors of young and old, the dog knew that this was a young man.

The dog padded silently through tall, wild grass growing beside the creek. He drooled at the odor of food, but because painful experience had taught him to be very careful in all dealings with men, he did not go any nearer. He licked his chops with a moist tongue and excitement danced in his eyes. How he would love to be near that fire, partaking of the food and the caresses of the young man!

But he had better be careful.

At the same time that the dog met the farmer who hurled the block of wood at him, Jeff Tarrant was walking down a dusty road that led into the town of Cressman. Two days past his eighteenth birthday, his face betrayed his youth. Healthy as sunshine, he walked with a spring in his step and his head held high. His rather loose lips formed a grin that seemed permanently fixed. His blue eyes sparked and a shock of curly red hair that needed cutting tumbled on his head. Even if it were not for the pack he carried, he would have commanded a second glance.

The pack, made of both canvas and leather and with straps at strategic intervals, was huge. It began at Jeff's hip line, extended two inches over the top of his head, and it was bulging. Across it, in black letters as big as the pack would accommodate, was:

TARRANT ENTERPRISES
Ltd.

Jeff himself had designed the pack to fit his needs, and he had done the lettering. It described him perfectly, for what nobody except Jeff knew was that Tarrant Enterprises was limited to whatever might be in the pack.

He walked cheerfully, for it was a cheerful day, and he gave thanks for the sparsely-settled country and the little-traveled road on which he found himself. In the first place, this was the only kind of country in which Tarrant Enterprises, Ltd., could flourish. Secondly, the day was made for walking. When Jeff found himself on traveled roads, he was forever being offered rides, and for the sake of both courtesy and good business he always accepted. But there had been no rides today.

Descending a hill, Jeff looked down at a junction of two forested valleys, up one of which a train was puffing. He looked at it closely, while the smile in his eyes and that on his mouth seemed to grow a little more pronounced. Railroad tracks meant

7

towns somewhere, and the sort of business Tarrant Enterprises, Ltd., could do in towns depended on circumstance.

Jeff sniffed deeply, for part of his success depended on an ability to sense what lay ahead, just as a hunter must sense what is in the offing. Now he had wood smoke in his nostrils, and he was not surprised when he rounded an outjutting corner of the hill and saw a farm house.

Jeff whistled happily as he approached the house and knocked on the front door, and he had the most gracious smile Tarrant Enterprises, Ltd., could muster up for the woman who opened it.

"Good afternoon, ma'am. I represent Tarrant-"

"Don't want nothin'!" she rasped. "Never buy nothin' from peddlers!"

Hard work, loneliness and collapsed dreams had all left their marks, so that she was almost as weather-beaten as the house. But Jeff saw at a glance that the place was neat and clean, and since she did not close the door, he entered, swung the pack from his back, and laid it on a table.

"Get it off!" she scolded. "Don't want no dirty pack on my table! Don't want nothin' from no peddler nohow!"

Jeff sniffed hungrily. A delicious incense, the mingled odors of roast chicken and fresh-baked bread, blessed his nostrils. He said slowly and with dignity,

"I am not a peddler, ma'am. I represent Tarrant-"

"Now, look! I just broke my parin' knife an' I got no time-" "Ah!"

Like magic, and seemingly without visible motion, the pack opened. From it Jeff took a paring knife with a gleaming blade and a shiny black handle.

"Only seventeen cents, ma'am. Blade of finest steel and hilt of genuine polished wood! Holds its edges and its temper, too! A lifetime knife!"

She looked at the knife, longing in her eyes. When she glanced again at Jeff, she was not so hostile.

"Got no money," she admitted.

Jeff laughed. "I asked for none! Our conversation became so fascinating that I had no chance to explain that I represent Tarrant Enterprises, Ltd. We have long recognized the needs of people such as yourself, people who prefer the refined quiet of country life to crowds and cities. But country life, as you must know, is not without inconveniences. Our only aim is to bring to the doors of people such as yourself whatever may not be available."

Her eyes were suspicious. "You mean you're givin' me this knife?" "Not at all, ma'am. Tarrant Enterprises, Ltd., is always willing to barter.

Umm! Is that roast chicken I smell?"

"I ain't tradin' you no roast chicken for no little knife!" "Surely one small knife will not fill your needs?" "Well, I could use some cinnamon sticks."

With the same magical ease, Jeff opened his pack and gracefully offered a small parcel of cinnamon sticks.

"Cinnamon from Ceylon," he said, at the same time wondering if he did not have cinnamon and tea confused. He went on, "The world's only pure cinnamon, made available to Tarrant Enterprises, Ltd., through special sources."

"My," she was impressed. "What else do you have?"

Jeff said, in the same tone that a department store manager would have used, "What do you wish, ma'am?"

She eyed the pack. "You wouldn't have some real nice gingham?" "Certainly."

Again it was as though the pack opened itself, and from it Jeff took a partial bolt of red-checked gingham. Her eyes softened.

"It's real pretty."

"Feel its texture," Jeff urged. "Tarrant Enterprises, Ltd., stocks only the best. Shall we say about six yards?"

She said doubtfully, "Best make it three."

Jeff whipped a pair of scissors from his pack and a folding ruler from his pocket. He measured and cut three yards of gingham. She fondled it dreamily, and compared to the dress she wore, it was elegance itself. Jeff stood expectantly, as though everything in the world were available in his pack.

"Anything else?"

She eyed the scissors. "Can I have them, too?"

Jeff frowned slightly. "I don't know, ma'am. They sell for a dollar and ten cents, and Tarrant Enterprises, Ltd., must show a reasonable return. Now-"

She said, as though suddenly remembering, "I've got a dollar." "And for the rest might we have bread and chicken?"

"Oh, sure! I'll get it right now!"

She ran into the kitchen, lingered a few minutes, and returned with a large package, one almost as large, and a small parcel. Jeff smacked his lips. The largest package could contain nothing less than the better part of a roast chicken, the one nearly as large must be a whole loaf of bread, and she pressed all three on him.

"Some butter for your bread, an' here's the dollar. You comin' through again?"

"When I do, ma'am, you have an honored place on my list of valued customers."

"Then you will stop?" "Most certainly."

"Be sure now."

"Ma'am, you have the word of Tarrant Enterprises, Ltd."

Jeff strode happily down the road, and he had cheated his customer in no way. Tarrant Enterprises was always ready to barter, for Jeff had long since learned that money must be spent. Now he had a meal as good as any the best inns served and he had it for half of what he would have paid in cash. But the woman was happy too, and that always made for a fair deal.

When he came to where the two valleys made one, Jeff left the road and sought the railroad tracks. Last night he had slept in a haystack, but it was far from an ideal bed. Jeff had not resented the mice, for he thought mice were interesting. The hay itself had been old, filled with seeds and thistles, and tonight he wanted a better camp. It was always possible to find one along a railroad.

As it always did when he sighted potential customers, Jeff's interest quickened when he saw two men with a handcar beside them, working on the tracks. He came abreast of them, two sweating, bewhiskered men who, even on this bright day, managed to look sullen.

"Good afternoon, gentlemen."

They glowered at him from beneath bushy eyebrows, and looked meaningly at each other.

"Beat it, peddler."

Jeff laughed merrily. "What a refreshing sense of humor! Such an intelligent bit of wisdom! You are just the men I hoped to meet! I represent Tarrant-"

"Beat it, peddler."

"Now just think about that! Reconsider! If-"

The two raised threatening pick axes. "Are you deef?" "I was just going," Jeff said hastily.

He was not so much as a trifle saddened as he trudged on down the tracks. Even Tarrant Enterprises, Ltd., could not overcome sales resistance that was backed by threatening pick axes, and nobody won every time. Nobody had to, for just down the road there were sure to be new customers.

Jeff came to a steel railroad bridge and looked with delighted eyes at the creek flowing beneath it. It was a clear, spring-fed stream, and it purled down riffles that filled a deep pool. Beneath the bridge there were weeds, sand, some big rocks, and driftwood.

Scrambling down the embankment, Jeff sighed at the sheer luxury of such a place. It had everything anyone needed. Carefully, he laid the pack down, put his food parcels in the shade, and from his own personal compartment of the pack he took a towel, a wash cloth, a bar of soap, a tooth brush and a comb. Taking off his clothes, he plunged into the pool and swam across. After five minutes he waded out, soaped himself from head to foot, and rinsed in the pool. He was thus engaged when the handcar rattled over the bridge.

Jeff dried himself, dressed and combed some order into the chaos of his hair. For a while he was satisfied to lay in the sun, happy just to dream.

Left without parents when a young child, he had been brought up in an orphanage which he had voluntarily left when he was fourteen and a half. He had worked for a farmer, for a livery stable which was in the process of becoming converted to a garage, for a pipe line crew and for others, long enough to convince himself that there is no special virtue in and not much to be gained through hard work alone. For the past two and a half years he had been owner, manager and entire working force of Tarrant Enterprises, Ltd.

That, by train, car, horse conveyance and on foot, had taken him to both coasts and both borders. He spent his summers in the north and his winters in the south, and the tidy roll of bills sewed in an inside pocket was proof that hard work is fine and wonderful if combined with initiative and intelligence. It was a happy life, one he liked, and though he thought he might take roots some time, he was not ready to do it yet.

Not until dusk brought the first hint of evening chill did Jeff gather wood and build a fire. He built it close enough to a big boulder so that the rock's surface would reflect heat, but far enough away so that it would not be too hot. He lingered beside the pool, listening to the night noises.

Out in the forest a whippoorwill began its eerie cry, and a sleepy bird twittered from its roost. The purling riffles splashed and called and a breeze set the forest to sighing. Only a stone rolling down the embankment seemed to be

out of tune. Jeff's fire cast weird shadows, and the snapping of the burning wood added its own notes to the symphony of night.

Jeff turned from the stream toward his fire and confronted the two men whom he had met along the railroad. Now he knew why that stone had rolled.

Except for this one small sound, they had come silently, and in the firelight they seemed even more unkempt than they had appeared in the full light of day. They were big men, all muscle, and they carried pick handles in their brawny fists. Jeff felt a cold chill ripple down his spine, for it looked as though the least Tarrant Enterprises, Ltd., was about to lose was its entire capital stock. He tried to take command of the situation.

"Good evening, gentlemen! I thought you'd be back! I was sure you are an intelligent-"

One of the men said, "Take him, Buff."

The two parted to come at Jeff from both sides. He looked longingly at a club lying near the fire, and as though he had read Jeff's mind, the man called Buff stood on the club. Jeff backed slowly toward the water. He might lose the pack. But he intended to keep his money and he had no intention of letting anyone work him over with a pick handle. As he retreated, he felt with his feet for rocks, clubs, anything at all with which to fight back. The two men advanced slowly, and Jeff risked a backward glance to see himself within three paces of the water. There was only sand beneath his feet.

At exactly that moment, the dog appeared.

He came slowly, with dignity, but uncertainly, because he was not sure of a welcome. Neither was he able to restrain himself any longer. For more than a half hour he had hidden in the grass, studying and entranced by Jeff. Now he had to find out whether he was acceptable. He halted four feet away, not caring to go any closer until he was sure.

Seeing him, Jeff saw his own salvation. He snapped his fingers and said, "Well! Where have you been keeping yourself?"

The dog sighed ecstatically. For so very long he had sought someone and now at last he had found him. He came forward to brush his shaggy back against Jeff's thighs, and he looked up at the two men.

Huge, a wild and savage-appearing thing, even in the full light of day, he was even more so by the fire's dancing glow. His eyes sparked. His pendulous jowls seemed taut and strained, and though he regarded the two men with suspicion only, neither could know that. They backed.

Jeff patted the big dog's head and said amiably, "Just my dog. Just my little old dog. I need some help while I attend to the far-flung business of Tarrant Enterprises, Ltd." His tone became slightly reproachful and he said to the dog, "Here! Here! Don't bite them now!"

The two men scrambled up the embankment and disappeared.

2. BAD LUCK

Where it flowed into the pool beneath the bridge, the creek made rippling little noises. A swimming muskrat, going upstream and suddenly seeing the fire and the two beside it, splashed as he dived. From somewhere up in the forested hills there floated an owl's mournful cry. Over all murmured a caressing little breeze which, while still soft with summer's gentleness, had within it a foretaste of autumn's cold.

Shaken, Jeff stood a moment. It was not the first time anyone had tried to strong-arm his pack away from him, but it was the closest anyone had ever come to succeeding. His fright ebbed away. Tarrant Enterprises, Ltd., had led him into other unusual situations and doubtless would lead into more. He turned to the dog.

"Welcome, Pal!" he said grandly. "From now to forever you may share the fortunes of Tarrant Enterprises, Ltd.! But what the dickens sent you at exactly the right time?"

The dog quivered with delight. He had wandered for so long, his only aim to find someone who would be glad of his company, and at last his goal was reached! He wagged a happy tail and licked Jeff's hand with the tip of a moist, warm tongue. Though he would never cringe, the dog would appease, and now that he had found someone, in order to stay near he would appease any way he could. Jeff's exploring hand found the dog's matted head and ears, and a puzzled frown wrinkled his forehead.

"Whoever you belong to hasn't been taking very good care of you," he murmured. "Haven't you ever been brushed?"

His hands dropped farther, to the dog's sides, and when he touched the right front shoulder the great animal winced and brought his head quickly around. Jeff had found the place which the chunk of wood had struck, and that was painful. But the dog did not bare his teeth or growl. Jeff took his hands away.

"You've been hurt, Pal," he said understandingly. "Here, let me feel it once more."

12

Very gently, pressing no harder than was necessary, he went over the right shoulder again. He could feel no broken bones, but just beneath the skin was a jelly-like mass of congealed blood, and when Jeff brought his hand away his fingers were sticky with blood. Next he found the wound inflicted by the brindle bull, and as he continued to explore his puzzlement increased.

The dog wore a round leather collar that formerly might have fitted well, but because he was thin, it now hung loosely. There was no license or identifying tag. Starved to gauntness, obviously the animal had been receiving neither food nor attention. His long fur was matted, and there were so many burrs of various kinds entangled in it that there was almost no hope of grooming him properly.

The conviction grew upon Jeff that this dog was a stray, and that he had come to the fire because there was no other place for him. Either he'd lost his master or the master had lost him, and in either event, he was homeless. Jeff frowned.

The whole success of Tarrant Enterprises, Ltd., hinged on its being entirely footloose. There were places to go, and often it was essential to go there in somewhat of a hurry. Obviously, it would be impossible to take a dog this size on a train, and certainly nobody with any sort of vehicle would be inclined to pick him up.

Jeff said good-humoredly, "Why the dickens couldn't you have been one of those flea-sized dogs that I might have tucked in my pocket?"

The dog wagged his tail and looked at this friendly human with happy eyes. Jeff rubbed his huge head and tried to think a way out of his dilemma. Surely the big fellow had no home and was loose on the countryside. Familiar with stray dogs, Jeff knew that just one fate awaited them; sooner or later, but surely, they were killed. Ordinarily the young trader would have confined himself to pity. But this dog had helped him when he was in desperate need of help. He must not be abandoned now.

Perhaps, Jeff thought, he could find a family that would give the dog a home-but he abandoned the notion almost as soon as it glimmered. How many families wanted a dog half the size of a Shetland pony? Maybe he could pay someone to take care of him. But how could he be sure that the dog would be cared for and not abused? There was no way to check. Six weeks from now, depending on where Tarrant Enterprises, Ltd., led him, Jeff might be a hundred or a thousand miles away. He did not know when, if ever, he would come back. The happy thought that first things must be first occurred to him.

While the dog looked gravely on, he tilted his bubbling coffee away from the fire and unwrapped the chicken. The dog licked his lips and riveted his gaze on the fowl. Jeff grinned. He'd been told that dogs should not have chicken bones. But unless they were always tied or penned, sooner or later most dogs found and ate them. At any rate, the dog had to eat and there wasn't anything except chicken, bread and butter. Jeff sliced both legs from the chicken and ordered,

"Sit!"

The dog sat; obviously he had had training. When Jeff extended a chicken leg, the dog took it from him so gently that only his lips touched Jeff's

hand, but when he had the leg in his mouth he tore all the meat from it with one turn of his jaws. Then he ground the bone to bits and swallowed that too. Jeff looked

13

at the two bites he had taken from his own drumstick.

"Hey!" he protested. "Just because you're company, you don't have to gobble everything in sight!"

He looked determinedly away and took another bite of chicken, but he felt the dog's appealing eyes on him and turned back again.

"If you could talk," he said resignedly, "you could be sales manager for Tarrant Enterprises, Ltd. You certainly know how to sell yourself."

Jeff cut a wing, gave it to the dog, and watched in fascination while it went the way of, and as fast as, the chicken leg. He cut the loaf of bread into six thick slices, spread an equal amount of butter on each, and saw the dog gulp five of them. Jeff ate as rapidly as he could; if he was going to get anything, he had to get it fast. He watched while the dog ate all the rest of the chicken and cleaned and swallowed the splintered bones.

"If you're going to be a partner," he observed, "you'd better learn to pay your own way. I'll go broke just feeding you. Oh, well, we can always have nice fresh air for breakfast. Now I'm going to work on you, Pal. You do look sort of wild and woolly and it might help both of us stay out of trouble if you didn't. Down!"

The dog lay down, eyes glowing happily, and Jeff used gentle fingers to untangle his fur. Where it was matted too tightly, he cut it off with a pair of scissors. Separating a hair at a time and using as little pressure as possible, he worked on the injured right side. Then he took a brush from his pack and brushed the dog smooth.

When he was finished, the animal still looked huge. His eyes sparked in the firelight and his flabby jaws loaned him an air of grimness. But his coat was no longer tangled or burr-matted. He looked forbidding enough so that it was easy to understand why the two track workers, seeing him and thinking he was Jeff's, had decided to run. Even though they were armed with pick handles, anyone at all might well hesitate to make rash moves around this mammoth creature.

"Now we have to get wood, Pal," Jeff told his new friend. "The nights in mountain country are apt to be on the cool side."

He cast around for driftwood that the creek had thrown onto its banks and when he had an armful, he dumped it near the fire. Always the dog padded beside or behind him, as though fearful he would lose this kind master should he wander more than a foot from him. Jeff threw some wood on the fire and a shower of sparks floated into the air. The dog curled contentedly near when he lay down with his back against the boulder.

Jeff awakened at periodic intervals to throw more wood on the fire, and in the misty gray of early morning he was aroused by the unmistakable sound

of a freight train making up. He listened intently; it paid to understand freight trains. He hadn't known how far off Cressman was, but he knew now. Judging by the sound of the freight train-the railroad yards must be in Cressman-it   was about one mile or twenty minutes' walk away.

Without getting up, the dog bared his gleaming fangs in a cavernous yawn. He rose, stretched, came to Jeff for a morning caress, and drank from the creek. Jeff looked admiringly at him. The dog was one of the biggest he'd ever seen, but he moved with all the grace of a much smaller animal. Jeff dipped water, prodded his fire and put fresh coffee on to brew. The dog looked expectantly at him.

"You ate it all last night," Jeff explained. "There isn't a thing left unless maybe you like coffee."

The dog sniffed about to lick up splinters of bone and Jeff looked at his big pocket watch. He lay back against the boulder, pillowing his head on his hands and blinking into the rising sun.

"Quarter to six," he told his companion. "And we have to time our arrival in this metropolis almost to the minute. Time waits for no man, but we'll wait for time."

The freight labored toward them, rumbled over the bridge and sent a shower of dust and cinder particles down. Sitting a little ways from the fire, the dog did not even look up. Jeff poured a cup of black coffee, sipped it, and the dog licked his chops. He was not as hungry as he had been, for last night's meal was a satisfying one. But he had been so long without food that he would have eaten had there been anything to eat.

Jeff still lolled idly against the boulder. Dogs were welcome in some towns and unwelcome in others, and Jeff had never been to Cressman. But it was a county seat, there was sure to be a court house, and court houses opened at nine sharp. Jeff wanted to be there at that time but not before. If the dog had a license, even though some might protest his presence, they could do nothing about it as long as he was accompanied by Jeff.

Finishing his coffee, Jeff poured another cupful, drank it and dozed for a while. Though he had had a long rest, it was well to sleep while he could. Often Tarrant Enterprises, Ltd., walked into a situation where there was no possibility of any rest. At exactly twenty minutes to nine, with the dog beside him, Jeff started down the tracks.

Cressman, he saw when he entered its outskirts, was a good-sized town and typical. Neat white houses framed both sides of the street. The business section would be farther on, and naturally the large building with a flag pole on top would be the court house. Jeff walked swiftly, paying no attention to the stares directed at him. He had expected the dog to arouse notice. The clock over its entrance pointed to nine when he reached the court house.

The dog close beside him, Jeff entered and turned down a corridor where a white-lettered black sign indicated that licenses might be had. He paused beside a grilled window behind which was draped a lank, black-haired, heavy-eyed, middle-aged clerk who looked as though he had never been fully awake. Without glancing around, the clerk asked a weary, "Yes?"

"I want a license." "What kind?"

"What kinds do you have?"

"Hunting, fishing, marriage, building, auto, dog, store, cafe-" "A wide-enough choice. I want a dog license."

Jeff took the yellow form and the pencil that were offered to him and started to write. He turned the pencil sideways and pressed until the lead broke. Jeff handed it back.

15

"This is no good. I'll use one of my own."

His hand stole into the pack and brought forth a mechanical pencil. Not looking at the clerk, Jeff gave absorbed attention to the yellow form. Under "sex" he wrote "male." When he came to "age" he looked shrewdly at the dog and penciled in "3 yrs." "Breed" proved difficult, but not for very long. Sure that nobody else would know it either, Jeff wrote "Algerian boar hound." "Name" was simple. Happily Jeff wrote "Pal" and shoved the slip back through the grill.

The clerk was staring intently at the pencil. "Where'd you get that?" "This?" Jeff held the pencil up. "It's a Bagstone, the newest thing. I
wouldn't be without one."

"Want to sell it?"

"Uh-uh. I have only a couple left and I may need them." "What's it cost?"

"A dollar."

"License is fifty cents. Can we swap?"

Jeff passed the pencil through the grill, but instead of the expected fifty cents, the clerk handed him another slip of paper.

"What's this?"

"Peddler's license and you're a peddler. They cost fifty cents, so we're
even."

Jeff, who had thought the clerk a narve rustic, grinned his appreciation
of someone else who knew how to get what he wanted and started down the corridor. He was still cheerful; he'd bought a dozen of the pencils for two dollars, and all except two were sold. It was a good sign, and he might do a brisk business in Cressman. He hadn't thought so when he came in because there were many stores, and usually people would not buy from a peddler if they could get what they wanted at a store. But Jeff felt lucky.

Coming in, he'd been in too much of a hurry to reach the court house to pay much attention to the town. Now he had an opportunity to examine it closely.

Between 2500 and 3000 people, he guessed, lived in Cressman. They were supported by the railroad yards and by a sawmill whose screeching saw made a hideous noise on that end of town which Jeff had not yet visited, and the workers must be well paid because there was every evidence of prosperity. The wooden sidewalks were well cared for, the dirt streets were clean, the horses on the streets were good animals that cost a fair amount of money, and there were a few autos with brass-fronted radiators.

These were all good signs. The fact that the stores seemed well patronized was bad, but Jeff wouldn't be able to tell until he had done some canvassing of his own, and he wanted to do that before getting breakfast for Pal and himself. Trade ran in cycles. If one Cressmanite was quarreling with the storekeepers, the chances were good that the person's friends would be similarly disposed to take an unkind view of merchants. If there were several such quarrels, Jeff might do a thriving business.

The young trader took an unobtrusive stand beside a store whose sign read "JOHN T. ALLEN, GENERAL MERCHANDISE." Beneath that, in smaller letters was, "The best of everything for everyone at the lowest prices." Pal sat down as close

16

as he could get and touched Jeff's dangling hand with a cold nose.

There were few people on the street, but that was to be expected at this hour. The workers would be working, the housewives taking care of their houses and the children playing. Jeff's eyes roved down the main street. He located and filed away in his mind the doctor's office, the dentist, the stores, the blacksmith shop, the livery stable and other business establishments. He knew where the sawmill was and he saw two church steeples. With few exceptions, all the rest would be homes. It was a good, substantial town, one of many such that Jeff had visited.

He looked with mingled wistfulness and amusement at a boy plodding down the sidewalk toward him. About eight years old, the youngster wore a faded shirt, torn pants, and had a dirty face that was lighted by bright eyes and a grin. He shuffled along, being careful to step only on the cracks in the sidewalk and kicking at small objects in his path. Then he saw the dog. His head went up, his grin became a smile, and he hurried to pause in front of Jeff and Pal.

"Gee!" he breathed. "Is he ever big! What's his name?" "Pal," Jeff answered. "Do you like big dogs, son?"

"I like all dogs. Does he bite?"

"Gentle as a kitten. Go ahead and pet him."

Pal stood, his head reaching almost to the youngster's shoulders, and wagged a welcoming tail at the hand stretched toward him. The boy tickled Pal's ears and smoothed his muzzle.

"Wish he was mine!" he sighed. "Don't you have a dog?"

"My paw," the boy said mournfully, "won't let me have one. Well, I got to go down to Skinner's and get Maw some sugar."

"Take this."

Jeff drew a peppermint stick from his pack and extended it. The boy took it with the same hand he had used to pet Pal and grinned his thanks. Jeff watched him skip down the street and sighed. He liked everybody, but he had an especially soft spot in his heart for children. Besides, it was good business. Should he decide to make a house-to-house canvass, he had already paved the way in at least one home.

Two women passed, going to the far side of the walk and keeping their eyes averted when they reached Jeff, and a man came from the opposite direction. Without seeming to, Jeff studied him.

About thirty, the man was slim and supple. Snapping black eyes and a pert waxed mustache betrayed his French origin, and from his quick, sure steps he was a woodsman. He swerved into John T. Allen's store and Jeff decided that he was a man of short temper. A moment later, that opinion was borne out.

"Sacre!" came an outraged roar. "You are a dog among dogs! A pig among pigs! You cheat the honest people!"

There came a snappish but calmer voice. "Take it easy, Pierre."

"Nev-air!" Pierre shouted. "Nev-air, and nev-air do I come back!" He bristled out of the store, turned to fling a final "Nev-air, pig!" back into it, and confronted Jeff.

"You know what he do?" he screamed. "I need the knife, the good hunting knife! For it he wants a doll-air and twenty-five cents!"

"Maybe they're worth that much."

"Non! Nev-air!" He looked seriously at Jeff. "You sell the hunting knife?"

"I do not compete with merchants."

"You sell the hunting knife?" Pierre repeated. "I-"

"Sell me the hunting knife!" "But-"

"This I demand! Sell me the hunting knife!"

With every show of reluctance, Jeff drew a hunting knife with a three-

inch blade from his pack. Pierre snatched it and his eyes lighted deliriously. "How much?"

"A dollar and twenty cents."

"Is good!"

Pierre pressed a rumpled dollar bill and two dimes into Jeff's hand, danced back to the store entrance and waved the knife as though he were about to go scalping with it.

"See!" he screamed at the storekeeper. "Dog! See! The pedd-lair, he do better than you! I have the hunting knife!"

Pierre stamped fiercely away and Jeff settled back to watch. But only for a moment.

The man who came out of the store was no more than five feet three and so thin that he seemed in imminent danger of collapsing. His nose, covering a fair share of his face, was oddly like a rudder. A few strands of blond hair clung precariously to his head and his eyes were furious.

"Did you sell that man a knife?" "Yes, I did."

Without further ceremony, but with a roar that seemed incapable of emerging from one so small, the storekeeper bellowed,

"Joe!"

It was a signal Jeff had heard many times in many voices that expressed it many ways. This was one of the occasions when Tarrant Enterprises, Ltd., had better move fast. The dog fell in beside him as Jeff started to run. He was too late, though.

It was as though the storekeeper possessed some magical quality that could conjure up images at will. Jeff's path was suddenly blocked by a burly two-hundred-and-ten-pound man who wore a gun, a constable's badge, an air of authority, and who had never wasted any time acquiring fat. He loomed over Jeff as a mountain looms over a knoll.

"What's up?" he demanded.

"This peddler," the storekeeper reverted to his customary snappish voice, "is interfering with merchants. He sold Pierre LeLerc a hunting knife."

"Did you?" the constable asked Jeff. "Yes, but I have a license."

"It's not one that allows you to peddle in business districts," the storekeeper asserted. "Jail him, Joe."

"You comin' peaceable?" the constable asked. "Or should I take you!" "Peaceable," Jeff answered hurriedly. "Always peaceable."

"Come on, then. Your dog got a license?"

"Look for yourself. Just sort of watch your hand." "That dog bite?"

"Not usually."

"See that he don't, huh?" "I'll see," Jeff promised.

He fell resignedly in beside the constable while Pal paced behind him. He thought ruefully of how little a feeling of good fortune could be trusted. Still, by no means would this be the first jail to have him as guest, and probably it would not be the last. He might as well make the best of it.

"Nice town you have here," he said companionably.

"Yeah," the constable was entirely willing to be friendly, "it's all right." "How long have you been chief of police in Cressman?"

"Nine years. Say! That's a good title! Chief of Police, huh?"

"You should call yourself that," Jeff asserted. "Do you have much trouble?"

The constable shrugged. "It depends."

"There's just one thing I wonder about," Jeff said. "I've met a lot of police in a lot of towns. All the rest had silver badges. How come yours is brass?"

"It was silver when I got it," the constable said ruefully. "Blame thing turned color on me."

"Why don't you polish it?"

"I do ever' night. Use soap and all. Can't do a thing with it." "Have you tried Blecker's Silver Polish?"

"What's that?"

"A polish for badges." "Never heard of it."

"Some store in Cressman should stock it."

"They don't. I've tried everything they have." He looked searchingly at Jeff. "Do you have any?"

"Yes but," Jeff laughed nervously, "you've already got me on one charge. I wouldn't care to be up on two."

"Let me see it," the constable urged. "I'd better not."

"I won't tell a person, and you have the word of Joe Parker for that. Come on. Let's sneak behind this fence and have a look." "Well-"

In the shadow of the fence, Jeff took a jar of Blecker's Unique Silver Polish from his pack, dipped an end of his handkerchief lightly into it, and carefully rubbed a small portion of the badge. As though by magic, the tarnish disappeared and bright silver gleamed where it had been.

"How much does that cost?" the constable breathed.

"Thirty cents a jar, but you've treated me so nicely, I'll let you have two for fifty cents."

"Thanks." The constable slipped the two jars into his trousers pocket, gave Jeff a half dollar, and said, "Guess we'd better get to jail."

"Guess we had."

The constable steered Jeff and Pal back to the court house but took them into the basement, instead of the main entrance. There were two windows with a desk beneath them, and behind the desk sat a gray-haired man with a friendly face but a weary smile. In the dimly-lighted corridor beyond were four jail cells.

19

The constable paused at the desk. "Hi, Pop," he greeted the jailer. "This peddler was peddlin' near stores. You tell him what to do with his dog and pack, huh?"

Without another glance at Jeff, Joe Parker turned and started back toward the entrance. Even as he walked, he industriously polished his badge.

3. ESCAPE

The jailer tilted his chair, clamped both hands behind his head, and looked steadily at the new arrival. Jeff stood still, sensing something here that had not been evident at first glance. Pop had a kindly face and a weary smile, but were they a mask? After a moment, he spoke.

"What are you doing here, boy?" "Getting in jail."

"You're a peddler?"

"I represent Tarrant Enterprises, Ltd. Now I have here-"

"Whoa! Whoa there! I see a lot of peddlers. My knife is all right, my watch is all right, I don't need tooth picks, tooth brushes, or anything else, and I haven't any family. How long have you been peddling?"

"Quite a spell."

"You ever been in trouble before?"

Jeff said blandly, "I've been in jail before."

"You're just a kid and I don't like to see kids in trouble," the jailer murmured sadly.

"How much trouble am I in?"

"You'll be kept until you can be brought before Justice Murphy. He'll fine you five dollars and tell you to get out of town."

"Can't I see him now?"

"Justice Murphy," the jailer said, "has gone fishing. He won't be back for a week."

"Then I'm to be your guest for a week?"

"It looks that way. Might as well get you checked in."

He took a pad of forms from the desk and balanced a pencil. In the proper places he inscribed Jeff's name, age, the offense with which he was charged, and other

20

pertinent data. He looked closely at what he had written, and from the dark cells in back came a shouted, "Hey, Pop! Who's the new tenant?"

"Shut up, Ike."

"Aw, bring him back, Pop. Bucky and me'd like to meet him."

"You two be quiet," Pop reprimanded the prisoner. Then he addressed Jeff. "Ike Wilson and Bucky Edwards-they finally got caught."

"What for?" "Stealing chickens."

Jeff looked unbelieving and the jailer's face became less gentle. For a moment he was almost stern.

"That's serious. It isn't a light matter." "I know."

"Then why did you look so doubtful?"

"It seems a few chickens are hardly worth a jail sentence."

"They're not, and neither is anything else, but some people never learn that. It just happens those boys weren't satisfied with one chicken. They got three thousand that anybody knows about."

"Whew!"

"They'll pay for it. Now, Jeff, I'll have to take your dog."

Jeff sparred for time. He had known other people in similar circumstances whose dog had been taken away, and half the time they'd simply disappeared. That they'd sickened and died was the usual story, but actually they'd been destroyed because it was too much trouble to take care of them. Outwardly, Jeff affected an air of supreme indifference.

"Sure," he agreed. "Go ahead. Just be careful. Pal doesn't like a lot of people and he bites whoever he dislikes. Better be careful he gets his regular feeding every day, too. That's four pounds of the best ground steak. He hates everybody if he doesn't get it."

"Yeah?" Pop was not at all friendly now. "Suppose he gets sick?"

"If I don't get him back-and in as good a shape as when he was taken away-I know a couple of good lawyers."

"Lawyers cost money."

"I have a certain amount of influence."

Pop rubbed his chin reflectively and stared at the window. "I suppose you could keep him in your cell if you want to pay for his board."

"I might," Jeff said, knowing he had won this round and that his chance shot had hit the bull's-eye. Obviously, for reasons of his own, Pop did not care to have any lawyers investigating anything. "How good a cell?"

Pop was all brittle now. "If you've been in other cells, you know how good. How old are you?"

"Old enough to land in jail. That tie you're wearing, Pop. It hardly befits the dignity of your position and-"

"I told you not to try to sell anything to me! Maybe, just maybe, we can think up some other charge."

"We'd buy if we had any money!" the man in the back cell yelled. "What's your name, peddler?"

21

"Jeff Tarrant, representing Tarrant Enterprises, Ltd. The most quality for the most discriminating people."

"What's that dis-dingus mean?"

"It means shut up!" Pop snarled. "You're a smart one, huh?"

Jeff said meekly, "All I know is black from white. I take my pack in the cell too, don't I?"

"No!"

"I know exactly what's in it," Jeff warned, "and I know just what to do if even a penny's worth is missing. Maybe I know what to do if nothing's missing."

"We can get tough, too." "I want that pack."

"All right. Keep it and come on."

Pal stayed very close to Jeff as Pop led them toward the cells. The two chicken thieves came to the front of theirs and clasped the bars with their hands. They were wholly delighted because, in his brush with Jeff, Pop had come off second best. Jeff grinned back at them.

"Hi, Jeff! Got anything to make our happy home happier?"

"Tarrant Enterprises, Ltd., has something for everyone and can please you. Here is a nice hack saw."

"I'll take that," Pop said.

"You'll take it for thirty-nine cents."

"Hand it over. You'll get it back when you leave."

"Well-" Jeff gave him the hack saw and the pair in the adjoining cell roared with laughter.

Pop asked, "Got any more?"

"Unfortunately, the hack saw department is understocked and our new order has not arrived."

"Get in."

Pop unlocked a cell and Jeff and Pal entered. The bars were in front only; the cells were separated by brick walls. Adjusting his eyes to the gloomy interior, Jeff saw two bunks with dirty mattresses suspended by chains that were attached to the wall. There was an iron stand upon which stood a chipped basin and a faded towel. Beneath the stand was a bucket. Pop slammed the door.

"I sleep in front," he advised. "I've got a sawed-off shotgun and I know how to use it. Besides, just trying to break out can mean six months in prison. Think it over."

"Sure." Jeff smiled.

Pop strode back to the desk while the two chicken thieves shouted raucous insults. Jeff lost himself in thought.

The situation had been quite obvious from the moment he entered the jail. Few towns had a full-time jailer for two or three prisoners-unless there were other factors involved-and almost without exception such factors existed only when there were certain affairs that would not bear close examination. The majority of Cressman's citizens probably were honest, hard-working people, but some of its officials were not. The fact that they could be dishonest only because the rest were indifferent to the way their town's affairs were conducted

22

did not change the situation. If he were one of the inside clique, Pop would have a better job, but he evidently knew enough so that he had to be given something in order to prevent his talking. Pop's reaction when Jeff expressed such utter willingness to take the matter up with an attorney-offered additional proof of this.

Jeff let his hand fondle Pal's head as he considered his chances. There was little possibility of breaking out by force and it would not be a good idea to do so anyway. As things stood, he faced a minor charge. Breaking jail was a major one. It was illegal to keep him confined for seven days without benefit of counsel, but that could be brushed over. They could always claim that they had held him on suspicion of some more serious charge.

Jeff sighed. He held a club over Cressman, but Cressman held him in jail. He scratched Pal's ears and murmured,

"Let it never be said that Tarrant Enterprises, Ltd., gave way to despair."

"What'd you say, Jeff?" Ike called. "Comfortable home," Jeff answered gaily.

"Counted the cockroaches in your private suite?" "Not yet."

"We got forty-seven," Ike said proudly. "One nigh as big as that dog of yours. What you got in your pack?"

"Candles?" Jeff suggested.

"Law! If Bucky and me had any money, we'd buy some."

Jeff took three candles, which he bought for a penny and sold for three cents each, from his pocket. He handed two of them and a half dozen matches around the end of his cell.

"A gift from Tarrant Enterprises, Ltd."

"Thanks, Tarrant what-you-call-it. We'll pay you soon's we've found us a fortune."

"I'll count on it," Jeff said.

He lighted the third candle, dripped wax from it onto the iron stand, and set it upright in its own drippings. By its flickering light, he examined the cell more closely. It was what he had expected. The floor was dirty, the mattresses only a little less so, and cockroaches scurried for cracks.

Jeff let his hand brush Pal's head again. Completely trusting, the dog wagged his tail and shoved his nose against his master's thigh. Dragging the mattress from the top bunk, Jeff laid it on the floor. Conceivably, even a dog would protest against sleeping up there.

Hunger reminded Jeff that neither he nor Pal had eaten anything since last night, and again he took refuge in the happy thought that first things must be first. He edged up to the bars and said softly,

"Ike."

"Yeah?"

"Where's the food come from around here?"

"The garbage can," Ike answered sadly. "Anyhow, that's what I think." "Can we get any other?"

"If you got money, you can ask Pop."

"Nothing like trying." Jeff raised his voice, "Hey, Pop!" "What do you want?"

"How about something to eat?" "It's not lunch time."

"How about some anyhow?" "Got any money?"

Jeff replied mournfully, "A few pennies that I've been saving for my old age. I can pay for it."

Pop came to the cell. "What you want?"

"Three loaves of bread and three half pounds of cheese." "Let's have the money."

"Uh-uh. Bring it first." "Show me the money."

Jeff held up two crumpled dollar bills. Pop walked to the entrance and there came the click of his key turning in the lock. Breathless silence reigned; this was a momentous occasion that must be properly observed. Ten minutes later the key clicked again and Pop came in with parcels.

"Three loaves of bread," he read from a slip, "eighteen cents. A pound and a half of cheese, thirty cents. And," he looked maliciously at Jeff, "four pounds of the best ground steak for the dog, one dollar."

Jeff grinned; his own words had backfired on him. He had intended to give Pal a loaf of bread and a half pound of cheese, to offer the same to those in the next cell, and to keep as much for himself. But he did not lose his aplomb.

"Exactly!" he exclaimed. "Just what I wanted! But I wouldn't think of paying in money when I can offer something of great value! Now-"

"Give me the money," Pop growled. "A dollar and forty-eight cents." "Oh, well, if you must be crass-" Jeff gave him a dollar bill and forty-

eight cents in change. "Give my pals in the next cell a loaf of bread and a pound of cheese."

"Thanks!" Ike said feelingly, and even the silent Bucky mumbled his gratitude. Jeff laid his pack on the lower bunk, put his food on the pack, and made two sandwiches with a half pound of raw ground steak between each. He spread a paper, scooped two pounds of steak upon it, and gave it to Pal. The rest of the steak he passed into the next cell.

"This," Ike exclaimed, "is as good as a hotel! Best grub I ever threw a lip over! Jeff, if ever you want a helping hand, you can count on me and Bucky!"

"I'll remember," Jeff promised.

He ate his two sandwiches while Pal licked thoroughly the paper in which the steak had been wrapped. Then he looked up appealingly and Jeff threw him a quarter loaf of bread. The rest of the food he put in his pack. He heard Ike's whispered,

"Jeff."

Jeff went to the front of the cell. "Yes?"

"You want to get out of here, I'll make like I'm sick. When that old fool comes in, Bucky and me will grab him and get his keys. We'll give 'em to you and you can beat it."

"What about you?"

"Ha!" Ike scoffed. "They can't do much more to us than they're already going to do!"

"Thanks just the same, but we'd better not." "You like this hole?"

"No, but there must be a better way." "There's none quicker."

"I know. Thanks anyway. Why don't you two get out?"

"We don't das't," Ike mourned. "How'd we know, when we got Bill Wheeler's chickens, that Bill'd call his seven brothers in? They're asettin' round the town, just waitin' for me and Bucky to break loose, and every one of 'em with a rifle. When Bucky and me go out of Cressman, we got to go with officers."

Jeff chuckled. "Too bad, Ike. But I don't want to break jail."

The day wore on. Grown accustomed to the candle light, the cockroaches came out of their cracks and scurried across the floor. This proved vastly intriguing to Pal, who watched them interestedly. He made quick little rushes, but the cockroaches always escaped. Jeff walked restlessly around the small cell. There had to be a way out because there was a way out of everything, but he could think of nothing.

Suddenly inspired, he called, "Pop!" "What?"

"I-I just wanted to see if you were still there." "Of course I'm here."

Jeff, who had intended to hold a five-dollar bill against the cell bars and indicate that it would be Pop's in exchange for freedom, abandoned the plan almost as soon as he conceived it because it was hardly consistent with the business policies of Tarrant Enterprises, Ltd., or with its standards. He must pay for nothing if he could trade, and there had to be something he could trade for release.

Bucky said fretfully, "Jeff." "What do you want?"

"Got anything in that pack of yours that'll help pass time?" "How about some music?"

"Anything!"

Jeff took from his pocket a small mouth organ with which he often beguiled the hours. He was happy again, and his smile glowed once more. He'd been thinking too hard. If he relaxed with the mouth organ for a little while, and cleared his mind, he would get some new ideas. By way of tuning up, he blew a soft note and the cell erupted.

Pal, who had been lying quietly on the mattress, leaped to his feet, pointed his head erect, and voiced a weird howl. It was not the cry of a dog but a banshee shriek, a wailing of lost souls and tortured beings, and it filled the room like a solid substance. Descending on a low moan, it stopped. Pal lifted his lips and snarled fiercely.

The two in the next cell gave way to hysterical laughter and Pop bustled from his desk.

"You'll have to keep that dog-"

He took a backward step as Pal snarled again. The mouth organ hidden in his hand, Jeff stood innocently. Pop stared.

"Why does he do that?" "I don't know."

"You'll have to keep him quiet." "I'll try," Jeff promised.

His blue eyes were dancing and his smile broadened. Some dogs were affected by sounds beyond those which normally came to their ears, and Jeff had never decided whether they reacted because certain noises grated harshly on their ears, because some sounds reminded them of a battle or other experience, or if they were merely inclined to be in tune. Obviously Pal was given to the latter sort of response.

Waiting until Pop returned to the desk, Jeff blew the same note as softly.

Pal responded with a whole chorus of shrieks that began on a tenor note and ascended to a high soprano. The echoes rolled back from the walls and seemed to bound forward again. It was almost an incredible thing that was promptly repeated when Jeff blew another note.

"Shut that dog up!" Pop shrieked. "I'm trying!" Jeff said desperately.

The door opened. Joe Parker came in. Jeff blew again, very softly, and Pal's immediate response filled the room. Their faces angry, Pop and the constable appeared in front of the cell and shouted to make themselves heard.

"Quiet!"

"What'd you say?" Jeff yelled.

"Quiet!" he shouted.

Pal stopped howling, but he stopped so abruptly that the constable still

"If you can't make that dog be quiet, I'll take him out of here!"

Pal voiced the snarl that followed his howling and both men stepped back. Joe Parker's hand dipped to his gun.

"You don't have to shout," Jeff soothed. "I can hear you. And I wouldn't shoot, either. The dog's mine, he can't possibly hurt you, and there are two witnesses who will prove it."

"Sure thing," Ike agreed happily. "Bucky and me are your boys!" "Make him stop yelling," the constable said. "People are standing on

the street, wondering who's getting murdered down here."

"Send them down," Jeff invited. "I represent Tarrant Enterprises, Ltd., and I might sell-"

"That dog has to stop yelling!"

Jeff shook a chiding finger at Pal. "Stop yelling!"

Pop and the constable left. Ike and Bucky chuckled. Pal sat down, expectant eyes fixed on the hand that held Jeff's mouth organ. He knew now where the sound originated, and he was ready the instant Jeff raised his hand. Pop and the constable, their faces entreating rather than commanding, came back.

"Can't you make him shut up?"

"I told him. You heard me tell him." "We can't have that noise."

"Why not?" Ike jeered. "Does it keep all the workers in the court house awake?"

"Judge Carlson's trying to work," the constable said. "He'll be working until nine tonight."

"Thought you said he'd gone fishing?" Jeff accused Pop.

"That's Justice Murphy. He hears all the cases where no more than fifty dollars is involved."

"Don't make the judge mad!" Ike chortled. "What if he gets real upset?"

"Can't you make him shut up?" the constable pleaded. "I'll try."

The two went back to the desk. A match flared there, and an oil lamp

cast its yellow glow into the corridor; apparently night was approaching. The constable left and Jeff pocketed the mouth organ. Five minutes later he brought it out again and once more Pal wrecked the silence. The door burst open, slammed shut, and Pop and the constable stood before Jeff's cell.

Joe Parker spoke, "How'd you like to get out, peddler?" "I don't know," Jeff said smoothly. "I like it here."

"Now look, why can't you be reasonable? We haven't got much on you and we're not mad at you. Ever'body's going to be plumb out of their minds if that dog howls down here for a whole week!"

"What's your proposition?" Jeff asked serenely.

"We'll leave you out, give you and that howling wolf pack ten minutes to get out of town, and start looking for you."

Jeff hesitated, scenting a trap and guessing that something besides Pal's howling was involved. Probably Pop had not been reticent about the new prisoner's willingness to consult attorneys. Jeff said finally, "And if you catch

me, you'll have me for breaking jail, too?"

The constable retorted grimly, "We don't aim to hunt that hard."

For a moment Jeff pondered, as though considering everything seriously. His face was solemn when he looked up.

"Nope," he said. "It's not enough."

Ike looked pained. "What do you want for getting out of jail?" "Pop owes me thirty-nine cents for a hack saw."

"I'll give the hack saw back," Pop offered quickly. "I don't want it. I want thirty-nine cents."

"Oh, for pete's sake!"

Pop took a purse from his pocket, counted out thirty-nine cents, and passed it through the bars. Jeff pocketed the money.

"What's the next town?"

"Stay right in the valley. Seven miles down, you'll come to Delview.

You can't miss, and heaven help Delview if they pick you up!" "Any other place?"

"North through the mountains there's Smithville. Better not try it, there's no direct road and those mountains are plenty rugged."

"Good town, though," Ike called. "That constable in Smithville, he minds his own business most of the time. So does most ever'body else. It pays, in Smithville."

"Wild place, huh?"

"Not wild," Ike declared. "Just sensible." "I'll go to Delview," Jeff decided.

"That's worse'n Cressman," Ike snorted. "They jail you there for lookin' cross-eyed."

"You got to go now," Joe pointed out. "You took Pop's money." "Open the cell."

"'Bye, Jeff," Ike called. "Me'n Bucky may be seeing you." "Take care of yourselves."

Outside, instead of going to the main street, Jeff slipped behind the court house. Two more moving shadows in a place of shadows, he and Pal

flitted past a cluster of lilacs and darted to a patch of trees. They threaded their way through the town, always alert and careful.

Again on the outskirts of Cressman, Jeff heaved a sigh of relief and walked swiftly down the road. Once more Pal had saved the day; apparently Pop and the constable had wanted only, and wholeheartedly, to be rid of them. Jeff felt a little saddened. The shining name of Tarrant Enterprises, Ltd., had become a little tarnished in Cressman. The concern had spent money and earned little enough.

Jeff was startled by the gruff command, "Wait thar!"

He halted. A man stepped out of the shadows, looked closely at him, pointed a sawed-off shotgun at the ground and said, "Go ahead."

Jeff thought of Ike and Bucky. Probably this man was one of the pickets waiting for them.

He recovered his cheer. There were always fresh customers down the road, but they would not be where Jeff had told Joe Parker he intended to seek them. It would be no difficult matter to send a message to Delview, and to ask the police there to be alert for a peddler accompanied by a huge dog.

At the first break in the mountains, Jeff left the road and started for the opportunities that must surely await him in Smithville.

4. THE CABIN

The rising sun turned the tops of the mountains to gold, and like slow-flowing water, sunshine crept gradually down the slopes. In a grove of pines, a chickaree came out of the warm nest where he had spent the night. Three inches from his nest, the chickaree paused on an outjutting stub.

A hawk winged through the pines regularly, and though it had always missed by a comfortable margin, it had struck three times at the chickaree. The pines were part of a marten's beat, and the marten had chased the chickaree several times. In addition, on their way to one place or another, various other predators wandered through the pines and few of them were averse to eating chickaree.

The chickaree held perfectly still, bright eyes glowing and small ears straining. Neither the hawk nor the marten were present, and the chickaree was puzzled because he could see nothing else. That should not be. Three big bucks were spending the season on this slope and every night they bedded in the pines. This

28

morning there was no sign of them.

Though he could neither see nor hear anything, the chickaree knew that something was present, if only because the deer were not. After five minutes, having assured himself that there was no immediate threat, the chickaree set out to find whatever he had sensed.

He scampered up the pine, leaped effortlessly into another, and took a different stand. Again he examined the grove. A smell of wood smoke tickled his nostrils and the chickaree knew that a man had come to the pines. That much discovered, he went into action.

He leaped to another pine, raced swiftly up it, and made a leap so long that the twigs upon which he landed bent precariously. A master of aerial travel, the chickaree paid no heed.

Three minutes later he found the man sleeping under a big pine. There was a huge dog beside him and a bed of glowing coals so arranged that the heat they cast enveloped both man and dog. The chickaree paused, anger in his eyes. He had squatters' rights in these pines and he lacked the remotest intention of sharing them with any man. Biting off a pine cone, the chickaree dropped it squarely on the man's face.

Jeff Tarrant came awake.

There was no lingering struggle to achieve complete wakefulness and no dropping back for another five minutes' slumber because Jeff had long since learned that that must never be. He had to awaken instantly, and at the least disturbance, because there was always a possibility that he might have to get up fighting, and he had a distinct impression that something had dropped on his face.

Swift glances in all directions told him that there was nothing except Pal near, and Jeff relaxed. Now he could attend to the ceremony of awakening. Jeff rubbed his eyes, yawned, stretched and rose. Rising with him, Pal saw the madly-fleeing chickaree; following the dog's gaze, Jeff saw it, too. Appalled by his own boldness, the chickaree was putting distance between Jeff and himself as rapidly as possible. Jeff grinned.

"So! He doesn't want us around either! Pal, seems to me that lately nobody has wanted anything to do with Tarrant Enterprises, Ltd.! Shame on them!"

Pal wagged his tail and made an enthusiastic attempt to lick his master's face. Jeff pushed him away; Pal's tongue was approximately the size of a dish towel and the consistency of sand paper. Not to be defeated, Pal got in a number of good licks on his friend's hand and Jeff chided, "Cut it out! I can wash myself!"

As he walked to a little runlet that trickled through the pines and washed his face and hands, Jeff thought of last night.

In the valley up which he had traveled, that runlet became a good-sized stream, with several deep pools. Having fallen into two of them last night, Jeff had discovered the pools the hard way. But he had achieved his purpose. It was not only possible but highly probable that Joe Parker and Pop had ideas which they hadn't bothered to disclose when letting Jeff out of jail. If they were able to catch him again, he would be charged with jail breaking. That meant six months, and six months was plenty of time to steal the pack's contents. However, even if they followed him into the mountains, they couldn't catch him.

A satisfying vision of the Delview police looking for him, and of Pop and the constable hopefully waiting, formed in Jeff's mind. He grinned happily. Even though he was stranded in a wilderness with no customers in sight, and no telling when he would find any, Tarrant Enterprises, Ltd., was in business again. Jeff took his watch out, saw that it had stopped, set it for nine o'clock, and wound it.

He might be an hour, two hours, or three hours, off. It made no difference. Tarrant Enterprises, Ltd., guided its fortunes by the circumstances of the moment and not by the dial of a watch or clock. Any hour of the twenty- four, or any minute of any hour, might present a precious and never to be repeated opportunity. Therefore, it was better to be alert for what the moment might present than to depend too heavily on any timepiece.

Last night he had been in too much of a hurry to think of eating, and when he had finally put what he considered an adequate distance between

Cressman and himself, he had been too tired. Now he took the remainder of bread and cheese from his pack and divided both in half.

"Chow time!" he said grandly. "Here, Pal, a wonderful breakfast!"

Pal gulped his portion. Jeff ate more slowly, and when he had finished the last crumb he was completely serene. It mattered not at all that he was completely out of food or that it was an unknown distance to the next place where he would be able to buy more. By all means, the future should be carefully weighed, but the future was a great and shining promise and lack of food a small inconvenience.

"Let's go!" he said happily.

A little breeze sang to him, the sun warmed him, and he was completely cheerful as he resumed his journey. This was a new and fresh experience, and as such it was to be treasured. Pal ran a hundred feet ahead, slowed to a walk, and further slowed to a stalk so deliberate that he moved at a snail's pace. He looked questioningly back at Jeff.

Jeff wrinkled his brows. In town, or even near other people, Pal had not moved more than a yard away. Here he would leave Jeff and that was entirely understandable. Naturally he would feel freer in the wilderness, but what did he want? Jeff halted.

"What's up, Pal?"

The dog stared hard at a copse of brush and for a moment Jeff remained still. Then he advanced slowly.

"Hope I'm not doing it wrong," he murmured. "I know you're trying to tell me something, but I'm too dumb to understand your language."

Pal stayed perfectly rigid until Jeff was within five feet, then went in to flush two grouse from the brush. They winged thunderously up and drummed away, and a great light dawned on Jeff.

If Pal had not had a former master, he would not have been wearing a collar, and obviously that master had lived partly by hunting. Scenting the grouse, Pal had been asking Jeff, as plainly as a dog can ask anything, whether or not he cared to shoot them. Jeff petted Pal and heaped praise upon him.

"Good dog!" he exclaimed. "That's the boy!"

Pal sighed ecstatically because he had pleased his master. He had already helped Jeff out of two difficult situations, and for that alone he deserved loyalty. Now it became evident that he would not be wholly dead weight. Jeff, who had learned something about dogs, reviewed what he knew.

There were various dogs for various purposes. Thus the bull was for fighting, the dachshund went into burrows and dragged out whatever sought a refuge there, the setter hunted game birds, the hound trailed, etc. Occasionally there was an intelligent mongrel that combined the functions of two or more such specialists. It was difficult to imagine Pal crawling into burrows, but he had already proven his ability to hunt birds. Would he do anything else?

It occurred to Jeff that he knew little about his new partner and until now he had had little chance to do any probing. Now there was every chance.

"Heel!" he ordered.

Pal fell in beside him, walking at his left and just far enough away so there was no danger of collision. Jeff was delighted; he had already discovered that Pal responded perfectly to other commands and must have had much training. Five minutes later there came an interruption.

Buzzing angrily through the trees, a bee made straight for Jeff. It danced up and down in front of his face, seeking a place to light. Jeff swiped at it with his right hand.

When he did, Pal bounded forward. Swift as a deer, and as graceful, he raced among the trees. With seeming lack of effort, he leaped high, the better to see what lay about him. Finding nothing, he looked back perplexedly.

"Come on," Jeff coaxed. "Come on, Pal!"

Pal returned and Jeff petted him fondly. Now he knew something else about the dog. A hand waved forward was Pal's signal to look for game. Jeff stored the knowledge away, pending the time it might be useful.

Pal ranged ahead and on both sides. Jeff strode on. The mountain had been steep, but its summit was a broad plateau covered with pine forest, and somewhere in the distant peaks that Jeff could see must lie the town of Smithville. Sooner or later he would get there, and if he needed two or three days, that was all right. He was enjoying the hike, and the farther away Smithville was, the farther he'd be from Cressman.

He stopped to rest at a pond that fed a stream and saw trout in the clear waters. Removing his pack, he opened the right compartment, and took from it a fishing line and a box of hooks. He tied a hook to the line, cut a pole from a copse of willows growing beside the pond, kicked a rock over and gathered up the fat worms beneath it, baited, and cast.

A dozen trout rushed the bait. One got it, and Jeff landed him. He continued to cast until he had nine trout. Jeff dressed them, washed them, took a grill and salt and pepper from the pack, and cooked his fish. Pal cleaned up all the heads, all the bones, and four trout. Jeff ate the rest, smacking his lips over them and entirely happy.

"This," he sighed, "is the way to live!"

They descended into a valley and were crossing a field when a rabbit flushed in front of them. White tail flashing, it streaked through the grass. Jeff waved his right arm and Pal raced forward. So effortlessly that he almost seemed to float, he overtook the fleeing rabbit and snatched it up. The rabbit dangling from his jaws, he trotted back and laid his game in Jeff's hand.

Jeff laughed in sheer delight. Almost always he canvassed the back country, because that was the only place where, usually, he could be pretty sure of doing good business. But he had been so interested in his customers that he

had had little time for the wilderness. Now there was an opportunity to see and observe, and he liked everything around him. He still wanted to wander, but if he ever did settle down, it would be in such a place.

The two camped that night in another grove of pines, not knowing where they were and not caring, and Jeff broiled the rabbit. It was stringy and tough, but hunger proved a powerful sauce and when Jeff chewed and swallowed the last few shreds of meat he felt as though he had partaken of princely fare.

"I wouldn't mind if this went on for a long while!" he told the contented Pal. "I like it almost as much as you do!"

He arranged a fire to reflect against a fallen tree trunk, slept soundly all night, and awakened with dawn. There was nothing for breakfast, but there had been nothing for a lot of breakfasts and it made little difference. Sooner or later they would eat, and this morning it was sooner.

No more than four hundred yards from their camp they reached a brawling little stream that raced frantically downslope. Again Jeff strung his tackle and caught trout. He laid them in the grill and was about to build a fire when Pal growled.

It was a sound so soft that nothing more than a few feet away would have heard it. Jeff looked quickly at the dog and glanced around the forest. He saw nothing. Pal was on all fours, straining into the wind, and he growled again. Again Jeff found nothing. Leaving the pack and fish, Jeff stole to a big pine about thirty feet away and crouched behind it. He whispered,

"Down!"

Pal lay down and Jeff continued to watch. Two minutes later he saw a man coming through the forest.

Very tall and very thin, the man was dressed in a sun-faded shirt from which half of the right sleeve was missing. Protruding from it, what could be seen of his right arm had been scorched by so much sun that it was almost black. His left sleeve was tied at the wrist. As dilapidated as the shirt, his gray trousers ended six inches above scuffed shoes, and an expanse of naked leg showed that he wore no socks. A luxuriant beard covered his face, and curly black hair dangled over his ears and down the back of his head.

In many parts of the country Jeff had seen other men who might have been this one's twin. Obviously a hillbilly, he carried a carbine as though it were a part of him.

He lingered behind a pine about fifty yards from Jeff's pack and for a full minute he regarded it closely. Then, making no noise whatever, he approached and prodded the pack with his foot. As he looked curiously at the grill of trout, Jeff spoke.

"That's mine, stranger."

The man whirled, shouldered the carbine, and put it down again. Jeff rose. Bristling, his lips slightly lifted, Pal stayed very near. Pal knew what Jeff could not; the man was Barr Whitney and presently he spoke.

"I wa'nt goin' to tetch it."

"I know that." Jeff had a customer. "I can see that you're an honest man. But I thought I'd better make sure first."

"Right smart idea."

Barr Whitney looked swiftly at Pal and glanced back at Jeff. His eyes revealed nothing, but he kept the carbine down. Expecting a flow of questions, Jeff was momentarily disconcerted when his visitor did not speak. Jeff glanced at the knife on his belt.

With a six-inch blade, the point of the knife was thrust into a deer-skin sheath and there was a six-inch guard that protected the cutting edge. Sparkling keen, the blade probably was made out of an old file and fitted with an ingenious hilt of deer antler. Jeff watched the knife for only a split second. Homemade, it was the work of an artist and Jeff knew of lowlanders who would pay a good price for it. But he must not let the stranger know this. Barr Whitney remained silent and Jeff said nothing. Often it was productive of the best results to fit his own mood to that of a potential customer.

Jeff flicked his pack open, took from it a clasp knife that was almost a small tool chest within itself, removed the trout from the grill, and arranged them on a slab of bark. He became absorbed in the grill. Opening the file on the clasp knife, he filed a sharp point from the grill's wire handle.

He closed the file, opened a long, pointed blade, and cut the fishes' heads off. As he did so, he brushed the grill with his trousers, caught a loose thread which was always kept purposely loosened, and snipped it off with the scissors that the clasp knife also contained. Carefully he worked with the awl blade, poking the cut thread back into place.

Barr Whitney watched silently, then said, "Give me leave to look at it." "Sure."

Without looking at the other, Jeff gave him the knife. He started a fire, laid the trout back on the grill, and started cooking them. Jeff seasoned the fish and asked, "Had breakfast?"

"Yup."

Jeff gave half the trout to Pal and gravely stripped the flesh from his own share. He gave Pal the stripped bones, went down to the stream, dug a handful of sand from it, and scrubbed the grill clean. Barr Whitney was still opening and closing the blade, scissors, awl, screwdriver, file, and fork that folded into the clasp knife's stag handle. He spoke,

"Good knife." "Yeah," Jeff agreed. "How much?"

"Six dollars."

Silence followed. Jeff, who had guessed that Barr Whitney was as likely to have six thousand as six dollars, made up his pack.

The other spoke again, "You swap?" "Maybe."

"For what?" "Your rifle."

The other jumped as though stung. Jeff, who knew that it's as easy to trade a hillbilly out of his hand as to separate him from his rifle, continued to work calmly. The pack, never cumbersome, could be made so when he wanted to gain time.

Barr Whitney asked, "Trade knives?" "Let's see yours."

Stripping the knife from his belt, Barr handed it to Jeff. Betraying nothing of what he thought, Jeff unsheathed the homemade weapon. Razor- sharp, it was exquisitely balanced and so finely made that blade of steel and hilt of horn flowed into each other as smoothly and as naturally as two placid creeks mingle their waters. Ordinarily Jeff was able to do little in towns and cities. But he could if he had merchandise like this to offer. Aside from being highly practical, the knife was a collector's item. Jeff handed it back.

"Guess not."

"What do ye want?" "Two knives like that."

Smirking faintly, Barr Whitney thrust a hand inside his shirt and brought out the twin to the first knife. Obviously he'd been wearing it in a shoulder sheath. He dropped both knives beside Jeff and for the first time there was a change in his expression. His eyes were gleeful, as though he'd been too sharp for a peddler, and he clutched the clasp knife firmly.

Jeff said in pretended disappointment, "Guess I talked myself out of that one."

"Guess you did."

"Well, I do sometimes. Which way is Smithville?" Barr Whitney pointed down a valley. "Thar." "How far?"

"A piece."

Without further comment, Barr Whitney turned and strode into the forest. Jeff shouldered his pack and looked at Pal. The dog stood erect, still faintly bristled as he looked after the departing man and Jeff wondered why. He shrugged. Some people just naturally roused a dog to anger and it was not important. Jeff started toward Smithville.

Ike had spoken highly of Smithville, and in Ike's eyes its virtue lay in the fact that people there minded their own business. What Jeff had seen bore

that out. Hillbillies were independent, not at all inclined to meddle in the affairs of others or to having their own investigated. Scornful of anyone who wore an officer's badge, they were quick to take violent action if what they considered their personal rights were violated. But usually they did not bother those who let them alone.

Jeff strolled in the direction Barr Whitney had indicated. Somewhere ahead lay Smithville, and Barr Whitney had given him a completely new idea. This could not be a wealthy land if the man Jeff had met was any indication of its riches. Shut off from the world and with little money, the hill people must of necessity do for themselves, and few of them were satisfied to have everything slipshod. It naturally followed that they would have brought handicraft to a high perfection. Jeff planned as he walked.

Seldom had Jeff even tried to peddle in any town larger than Cressman; in big cities he could do no business at all. But not all of the people in cities were contented with the monotonous sameness of the stamped and stereotyped products available to them. They had lost the art of handicraft themselves, but some still appreciated it and were able to pay for it. On the other hand, there was an excellent chance that the inhabitants of these mountains, lacking the money to buy city goods, would be eager to trade for them. Jeff began to whistle.

"Pal," he said happily, "maybe, just maybe, Tarrant Enterprises, Ltd., is about to become an even bigger business!"

Pal was padding ahead, glancing from side to side and making eager little excursions into the brush and forest. This was his country. Times without number he had walked through these same woods with Johnny Blazer. Returning excited him. He went from a boulder to a patch of brush, and from there to a stump. His tail wagged constantly as once again he saw all the old landmarks that were so familiar and so dear. Not understanding, Jeff wondered. They came to a foot path. Jeff followed Pal down the path, not knowing where it led but sure that it would take them somewhere. If it did not bring them to Smithville, it would certainly lead to some house whose inhabitants could tell him exactly how to get there, and Jeff was in no hurry. He was naturally footloose and the woods were free. Jeff knew a mounting disinclination to go to Smithville at once. It would suit him better to camp in the open again tonight.

The path joined a road. There were wagon tracks, hoof prints, and even tire tracks left by venturesome drivers of automobiles. Jeff came to a sure sign of the latter, a blown tire lying beside the road, and shook a sympathetic head. He did not share the views of those who proclaimed cars a passing fad. They would be the conveyance of the future if only because they could travel as far in one hour as a horse could in three. Their many faults were sure to be corrected.

Pal frolicked like a puppy, ears shaking and tail wagging as he bounced around with a wide canine grin on his mouth. When he came to another dim foot path leading out of the woods, he halted to look inquiringly back at his master. Hesitantly-he had not yet had any assurance that Jeff wanted to visit it

-he looked longingly toward Johnny Blazer's cabin.

Wondering what Pal wanted now, Jeff halted beside him. The cabin was hidden by trees; from this distance no part of it could be seen. Then a puff of wood smoke drifted to Jeff's nostrils and the cabin betrayed itself. With Pal dancing eagerly ahead, he started up the path.

Fifty yards from the road, he came to Johnny Blazer's cabin and halted uncertainly. The place looked abandoned. Of the two windows he could see, a pane of glass was missing from each. Still, smoke drifted from the chimney. Obviously someone was living in the cabin.

Jeff knocked on the door. Nobody answered. He knocked again, and when there was no response, he walked in.

A homemade chair with one broken leg lay upended on the floor. There were a few broken dishes, a stove, scattered papers and dust. Wind blew through empty panes where glass had been. About to go farther in for a closer inspection, Jeff was halted by a near hysterical command.

"All right, mister! Raise both hands and raise 'em high!" "Certainly," Jeff agreed pleasantly. "Anything to oblige." Jeff raised both hands and heard, "Turn around!"

He turned to confront the yawning muzzles of a double-barreled eight gauge shotgun. Holding it and dwarfed by it, but never flinching, was a blazing-eyed boy who could not possibly be more than ten years old.

5. DAN

The boy stood about ten feet away, near a pot-bellied wood stove behind which he probably had been hiding when Jeff came in. His clothing was rumpled, but at the same time it was fairly new and not the faded hand-me- downs that were to be expected on ten-year-olds around Smithville. His face and hands were dirty, and straight black hair that had once been well-groomed tumbled all over his head.

Jeff knew a surge of pity. Never, in hill or any other country, should a ten-year-old stand so. It was not right that any youngster's eyes should spark with such unbridled fury, or that any child should have the complete willingness to kill that was so evident in this one. At the same time, Jeff felt something else. The youngster had control of himself and the shotgun did not waver. But taut lips seemed ready to tremble and tears lingered behind angry eyes.

It was as though the boy had taken up burdens which were far too heavy, but which he was determined to carry, even while he longed for a friendly arm to help him and a sympathetic ear to which he might tell his story. And somehow, in spite of his anger, quality was evident within him.

Jeff said gently, "Put your gun down, son."

"Tell me what you're doing here! With my pop's dog!" Jeff was astounded. "Your pop's dog?"

"That's him! That's Buster!"

Hearing the name, Pal flattened both ears and wagged his tail. He looked at the boy without going near him. Jeff tried to collect his thoughts.

"I found him a long ways from here. Clear over beyond Cressman." Uncertainty

36

stole some of the boy's fury. "You-you did?"

"That's right." "Who are you?"

"My name's Jeff Tarrant and I'm a peddler. Put your gun down."

"Well-" He lowered the shotgun. Two tears broke from his eyes and he shook them off with an angry whirl of his head. Jeff extended his hand.

"Maybe you'd better let me have the gun."

"It-it isn't loaded. I didn't have any money to buy shells!"

Jeff said gently, "Taking a bit of a chance, weren't you? What if you'd pulled it on someone with a gun that was loaded?"

"I-I don't know."

"This is really your dad's dog?"

"I ought to know him."

"He doesn't seem especially happy to see you."

"I-I only saw him twice. Last time a year ago. But it's my pop's!" "Who are you, son?"

"Dan Blazer."

"And where is your pop?"

"Dead!" Dan said fiercely. "Shot by those-Whitneys!"

He whirled so that his back was to Jeff, put both grimy hands to his eyes, and shook with sobs. Pal looked worried. Jeff strode swiftly across the floor, knelt beside the sobbing youngster, gathered him up, and sat with him on a homemade wooden chair whose back and seat were of laced buckskin. Laying his head on Jeff's shoulder, Dan sobbed unrestrainedly. Then he wriggled, turned away quickly so that Jeff could not see his face, and slid to the floor. He wiped his eyes with a handkerchief that was almost as dirty as his face. When he turned again to Jeff, he was calmer.

"Cry baby!" he accused himself. "Big cry baby!" "Come here, Dan," Jeff said gently.

"What do you want?"

"To talk to you, and I've seen men cry over a whole lot less." "Really?" The thought seemed a reassuring one.

"Really. Where is your mother?"

"She died when I was-When I was just a child." He spoke quietly. His mother had died so long ago that all pangs were gone.

"I see. What were you doing when these-uh-when these Whitneys shot your pop?"

"I was in Ackerton." Dan named the nearest city.

Again Jeff was surprised. "What were you doing there?"

"Pop sent me to Jackson School there. Said he was a hill man but he didn't want me to be one. He said there were better things."

"Hm-m. How did you get here?" "Walked," Dan answered matter-of-factly. "Didn't anyone try to stop you?"

"A policeman did before I was out of Ackerton. I got away, and after that I walked at night."

"Do you have any relatives?"

"I'm the only one left in the Blazer family and I aim to kill every danged Whitney! That way I'll be sure to get the one who got Pop!"

Jeff said drily, "Nothing like being thorough. You're sure the Whitneys did get your pop?"

"They're the ones he fought most with." "But he fought with others too?"

"Well, yes."

"Hadn't we better do a bit of thinking before we shoot all the Whitneys?"

"We? Why do you want to mix in?"

"I've got your pop's dog, haven't I? That gives me the right, doesn't it?" Dan looked doubtfully at Jeff. "Do you really think so?"

"Certainly I think so, but let's not go off half-cocked. This is going to take a bit of figuring. We can't just wander around leaving corpses all over the woods."

"What would you do?"

"Find who really shot your pop and get him." "I never thought of that," Dan admitted.

"Let's talk about it over a good meal. That sound all right?" "Great but-I'm down to corn meal mush."

"Tonight we'll have something else," Jeff decided. "I was just going in to Smithville to buy grub. Do you like pork chops?"

"Oh, boy!" Dan licked his lips. "But why should you buy me anything?"

"If we're partners," Jeff said firmly, "we share and share alike. You can understand that. We're already sharing the cabin."

Confidence and hope warmed Dan's eyes. He smiled, and Jeff reflected that that was the way he should always look.

"Uh-Jeff."

"What's up?"

"Do you think you could bring some shells for this shotgun?"

"On one condition. The gun isn't shot at anything, or anybody, unless both of us know about it."

"All right," Dan agreed.

Pal went to the door with him. Jeff shoved the dog back, shut the door, and struck into the gathering twilight. He shook a bewildered head.

Was it a year ago, or only a few days, that he had been the footloose owner-manager-working force of Tarrant Enterprises, Ltd.? Why was he burdened now with a dog that few other people wanted and a boy that nobody wanted very much? Why hadn't he left both where he found them and accepted just his own responsibilities? He shook his head again and murmured to himself, "Darn fool! Tarrant, of all the pinheaded things you've ever done, these take the hand-polished railroad spike!"

At the same time he knew that he couldn't have done otherwise. The dog had helped him, therefore the dog must not be abandoned. Nor could Jeff simply leave Dan to any fate that awaited him. The only man left in the Blazer family, Dan had walked all the way from Ackerton-more than a hundred miles to avenge his father. He intended to make sure he did it by shooting all the

Whitneys, and he would die if he raised the gun to the first one. It was a staggering situation and how should he, Jeff, solve it?

Again Jeff gave himself over to the idea that first things must be first and walked into Smithville.

It was a small town, with perhaps four hundred inhabitants, and as nearly as there could be such a thing, it was a place where the outer world intruded on the hills. Smithville was about half-civilized. The streets were dirt and rutted, but instead of the log houses in which hill families abode, the dwellings here were frame. The Smithville Inn was largely a place for those who wished merriment in its louder forms, and there was one store. Wagons piled high with logs offered mute testimony as to the way the town's residents earned a livelihood but there were no horses to be seen. Doubtless, with night approaching, the teamsters had stabled their draft animals.

Jeff halted in front of the store, a rather large building whose front end consisted of numerous small panes of glass inserted in wooden frames. There was the legend "Abel Tarkman, General Store," and beneath it was printed, "Post Office Too."

Knowing before he did so what he would find, Jeff entered. Isolated stores such as this one catered to all the wants of many people. As a result, they had to stock a little bit of everything that was practical, and Abel Tarkman's store was no exception. Counters stretched its full length. Pails, straps, lanterns and bits of harness, were suspended from rafter beams. There was a rack of hoes, rakes, spades and other garden tools, but no plows or harrows; this was not a farm community. Jeff saw a shelf of drugs, a vast assortment of chewing and smoking tobaccos, a whole rack of vari-calibered firearms and ammunition, a food counter, a dry goods counter, and toward the back-a small cubby hole of unpainted lumber that was labeled "Post Office."

Two other people, a stocky man with a badge, and a woman, were in the store. Jeff stood aside while the proprietor, evidently Abel Tarkman himself, served the woman. A small, quiet man with an inoffensive manner, he wrapped the woman's purchases and looked inquiringly at Jeff.

"Four pounds of pork chops," Jeff said.

He ordered a dozen eggs, two loaves of bread, a three-pound slab of bacon, two quarts of milk, a pound of coffee, a peck of potatoes, and mindful of the youngster at the cabin, a head of lettuce and a bunch of carrots. To these purchases he added a broom, four panes of glass to replace those broken out of the cabin, putty with which to hold them, a lantern, a gallon of kerosene, and finally, "A half dozen eight gauge shotgun shells."

"I've nothing but number fours in eight gauge." "They'll do and I want to stick them in my pocket."

Abel Tarkman looked doubtfully at the rest. "It's a lot to carry." "Put it in gunny sacks. I'll manage."

Tarkman reached beneath the counter for a gunny sack and said amiably, "Fishing?"

"Loafing," Jeff answered. "Nothing strenuous." "Staying long?"

"I don't know." "Where you staying?" "Blazer's cabin."

Abel Tarkman's jaw tautened and he said no more. Jeff frowned. It was as though something cold had crept between them, and why should the mention of Blazer bring that about? Without speaking any more, the storekeeper totaled Jeff's bill on a piece of brown wrapping paper and Jeff paid in cash. Ordinarily he'd have tried to barter, but, though the pack was full, he still had ideas about trading with the hill people.

Shouldering two half-filled gunny sacks, Jeff left the store. The sun had set, but enough light remained so that he could see. Between two far- spaced houses, and a sufficient distance from the store, Jeff took the six shotgun shells from one pocket and a knife from another. Carefully he pried the wadding from each shell and poured the shot out. Just as carefully replacing the shot with tightly-rolled bits of paper that he tore from his packages, he re- assembled the shells. Not forgotten was the fury of which Dan was capable. He had promised Jeff that he'd do no shooting on impulse, but Jeff wanted no accidents should Dan encounter a Whitney when he had the shotgun in his hands.

Jeff was reassembling the last shell when, his badge shining in the day's last light, the man he'd seen in the store came to and paused beside him.

"Howdy."

"Howdy."

"My name's Ellis," the constable said. "Bill Ellis and I'm constable
here."

"Jeff Tarrant," Jeff extended his hand. They shook and Bill Ellis asked,

"You said you're staying at Blazer's cabin?" "That's right."

"See anything of a youngster thereabouts?" "You mean Dan Blazer? Yes, he's there."

"Then I guess I'd better walk out with you and pick him up. Poor little tad's all alone in the world."

"No, he isn't. I'm taking care of him." Bill Ellis was suspicious. "Since when?"

Jeff managed to sound more than a little astonished. "Didn't he tell
you?"

"All he did was walk through Smithville yesterday with a little sack
over his shoulder and a shotgun big's a cannon in his arm. All he said was that
he would meet somebody at the cabin. I waited this long to see if he really would."

Jeff gave thanks for this bit of coincidence. "I met him at the cabin and he's all right. He's getting everything a youngster should have, though of course if your official duties call for so doing, you may take him. Naturally, I'll have to go with him and bring him right back, so there may be a bit of trouble. You were going to take him to an orphanage, weren't you?"

"Where else?"

"Ah, yes," Jeff agreed. "Where else? Splendid place, an orphanage.
Ideal for those with no one to whom they might turn."

"I got a letter from some school in Ackerton. Said the kid left there right after his dad's funeral and hasn't been seen since. Said they thought he'd come here and I should be on the watch for him."

"An error," Jeff murmured. "Why don't you write to the school?" "Maybe I'd better."

"Do that," Jeff urged. "How long does it take a letter to get to Ackerton and a reply back here?"

"About a week."

Jeff made up his mind to visit Ackerton before the week was out-and maybe Bill Ellis needn't send his letter.

"I'm going to Ackerton," Jeff said. "I'll bring written confirmation from the school if you want it."

"Well, if you're going there-"

"Let's leave it that way," Jeff said quickly. "If you care to check in the meanwhile, you can ask Dan. Who killed his father, anyway?"

"If I knew, he'd be in jail." "Haven't you any ideas?"

"Sure I have. It's one of maybe twenty-five or thirty people." "Have you questioned them?"

"How well are you acquainted around here?" "I just got in."

"That explains it then." "Explains what?"

"Your not knowing why I haven't questioned twenty-five or thirty people. Let me tell-"

Bill Ellis spoke at length of those who lived in Smithville and those who abode in the mountains surrounding it. The town dwellers, with few exceptions, were industrious people who were glad to work for the lumber company and to accept a weekly pay check. They seldom caused trouble.

Those residing in the hills were a different breed. They worked when they felt like it, which was not often, and few of them could bear the yoke of a steady job for more than three weeks at a time. They did for themselves and

took their living from the wilderness. Of late years, with hunters and fishermen finding their way into the hills, guiding them had become a good source of income. But the only reason the hill people were willing to guide was because they usually spent all their time hunting or fishing anyway. They made their own laws, lived by their own code, and united only when outside forces threatened any part of their way of life.

When they fought, they fought hard and often for little reason. For many years a feud, with the Whitneys on one side and the Paynters on the other, had raged. It had started, of all things, over a muskrat stolen from Jed Paynter's trap. His own judge, jury, and executioner, Jed had shot Enos Whitney. Two days later Jed was found with a bullet in his head and, though everybody knew one of the Whitneys had shot him, nobody had ever proven it. Finally, with four Paynters and two Whitneys dead, the remainder of the Paynters left the hills. No officer had ever proven anything. One who'd gone into the hills had simply disappeared.

Bill Ellis knew only that someone had shot Johnny Blazer. But who? Johnny had done well trapping, hunting medicinal roots, and guiding and boarding hunters and fishermen. There was not a man in the hills who wouldn't have liked what Johnny had and not a man who wouldn't have quarreled with him about it. But to go into the

41

hills with wholesale accusations would do nothing except rouse fury. Accusing, or even suspecting, whoever had not shot Johnny would be insult of the deadliest sort and inevitably bring on shooting.

Far from being interested in local quarrels, the outside world seldom even heard of them and little help could be expected from anyone. If Bill Ellis knew who had shot Johnny, he would go get him. But he had to know and had to have indisputable proof before he moved. He'd already done everything he could and was no nearer a solution than he had been two months ago.

Jeff listened intently, and realized that he was hearing the truth. If it was more extreme than what he already knew about mountain dwellers, Smithville was more isolated than any other place he had ever visited. Jeff thought of the youngster in the cabin. Dan Blazer had attended a city school, but his were hill blood and hill traditions. He had asked no one to help him avenge his father, but vengeance was a point of honor.

Jeff gritted his teeth. Dan was a child. It would be the essence of simplicity, using force if necessary, to place him in an orphanage or make him go back to school. But it would solve nothing. A boy now, Dan would be a man. When he was, he'd be back here in the hills. There would be no forgetting.

"Where was Johnny found?" Jeff asked.

"Between here and his cabin. If you noticed a big sycamore right beside the road, he was lying against the trunk."

"Who found him?"

"Couple of fellows from Ackerton. They were fishing back in the mountains and they brought Johnny here. Mike Severance, he does first aid work for the lumber company, patched him up and they took him to Delview. He died in the hospital there. Bullet went right through him."

"Where is he buried?"

"In Delview." Bill Ellis narrowed his eyes. "Who are you?"

"A peddler," Jeff answered honestly. "I thought I could do some business here."

"You will, too. Now tell me straight why that kid came back." "I told you. He's with me."

"We'll leave it that way," the constable promised, "at least until you bring word from Ackerton. But if you have any ideas except peddling, you'd better get some shells that are loaded with something besides paper wads."

"I'll think about it."

Bill Ellis guessed, "The kid toted the gun. Does he want the shells?" "That's about it."

"You aim to watch him?"

"Why do you think I'm giving him blanks?" "Why do you bother with him?"

"I'm an orphan myself. I could have used somebody to look after me when I was ten years old."

"For pete's sake, be careful!" "I'll keep that in mind."

"You know where to find me if you need advice," Bill Ellis promised. "But if you start any half-baked ruckus, you finish it. I've a wife and two kids to think about.

Well, maybe I'll be seeing you."

Pocketing the shells and shouldering the gunny sacks, Jeff walked swiftly back up the road. He halted when he came to the big sycamore. It was a monstrous tree that shaded the road and murmured gently as the evening breeze danced through its branches. There was nothing whatever to show that a man had died violently beside it. But a man had died here, and Jeff looked quizzically at the tree. If it could talk, it probably could tell who had killed Johnny Blazer.

He left the tree and hurried along. Trees did not talk and-Jeff was deep in thought until he came to the cabin. There he brushed his frowns away and forced a sparkle back into his eyes. Dan was a ticklish problem, and like all such, he had to be handled delicately. There must not be even one wrong move. Jeff burst into the cabin with a cheerful, "Poke the fire up, Dan! There's pork chops for supper!"

6. VISITOR

Sleeping in the same corner where he had slept so many times, Pal moaned softly and twitched his paws. He dreamed that things were as they had once been and that he was hunting grouse with Johnny Blazer. Pacing ahead, Pal scented a grouse and showed Johnny where it was. There came the shotgun's blast. The dream faded and Pal woke up.

Instantly things resumed a normal perspective. The scent of Jeff Tarrant filled the cabin and mingled with it was the odor of Dan Blazer. Pal remembered meeting Dan before. Every summer, but never for more than ten days at a time, Johnny had brought him to the cabin for a visit.

Though Pal liked all children, he saw only an incidental connection between Johnny and Dan Blazer. However, if only because Johnny had once welcomed the boy and Jeff was now welcoming him, Pal was happy to accept Dan too and to include him in the select circle of intimates who deserved every courtesy. Next to Jeff, he would respect Dan.

Though his nose told him that all was well, Pal did not go back to sleep at once. The dream had been a very vivid one and it brought a surge of memories that were strengthened by being back at his old home. The past remained a puzzle. Pal had never understood why Johnny had disappeared, he still did not understand, and he was troubled because of it.

Having a dog's instinct for time, he knew that the night was about half gone, and because he was familiar with the habits of humans, he was aware that Jeff and Dan probably would not get out of bed before sunrise. Equally at home in daylight or darkness, Pal had never known why people preferred to spend the night hours in a cabin or shelter but he had never questioned their doing so. They were humans. He was a dog. Therefore, it always befitted him to shape himself to their ways and never even think that they should bend to his.

Sometimes Johnny had taken him out at night to hunt coon, and Pal rather hoped that Jeff would do the same because he liked to run at night. But it would be all right if Jeff did not.

After a short time, needing contact more intimate than his nose offered, Pal rose and padded across the wooden floor. He ascended the steps, walking quietly because experience had taught him to be quiet. Pal existed to please his master and his whole life must be shaped to that purpose. There were no delights which, directly or indirectly, were not connected with that. When Johnny had patted his head and praised him, Pal had quivered with joy. Now he reacted in the same fashion to Jeff and his life was a full one.

He ascended the steps, walked to the bunks that Jeff and Dan occupied, sniffed gently at each, and went back to his place in the corner. He had made doubly sure that Jeff was still present and that partially satisfied him. But because the dream and the cabin brought Johnny back to him, he was still able to sleep only fitfully. Pal recalled last night.

He had been very worried when Jeff went away and left him in the cabin. Ordinarily it would have been routine, for Johnny had often left him alone. But a great fear had grown out of Johnny's death. Pal had seen him leave and been sure he'd come back, but he never had. Now he was fearful that Jeff might not return. Dan, who understood, had tried to give him comfort.

"He'll come back. Don't you worry. He'll come back."

But Pal would not rest until Jeff's return and then he was happy again. He wagged his tail because the two in the cabin greeted each other gladly, and he drooled at the odor of frying pork chops. Eating his share, Pal looked puzzled when Dan started to wash the dishes and Jeff began to work with the broom.

In Pal's opinion the cabin was satisfactory, and he had never understood the quirks of humans that kept them forever doing something that did not look like fun and seemed unnecessary. But Pal resigned himself to the cleaning up. He flattened his ears and retreated into a corner. He dodged from place to place whenever the broom came near, and relaxed in his own corner only when Jeff finally put the broom down and started replacing the broken window panes. Unoccupied, and thought deserted, the cabin had been rifled of many things belonging to Johnny. But there were enough dishes and tableware left, for Johnny had kept a great store of it to provide for his guests.

Dan yawned and Jeff sent him to bed, but the young peddler worked for a long while afterward. Finally, giving Pal a pat on the head, he too sought one of the upstairs bunks.

Now Pal raised his head at frequent intervals. He had a great yearning to visit again the sycamore tree-the last place where he'd seen Johnny, but the door was locked. If the customary routine was followed, it would not be opened until Jeff and Dan got up. Rising, Pal walked nervously around the cabin, sniffing at all the objects he knew so well. He went to his corner and did not leave it again until dawn's thin light turned the cabin's black windows to pale gray.

He heard a bunk creak as Jeff moved, and raised expectant ears. For a short interval there was silence. Then came Dan's sleepy voice.

"You awake, Jeff?" "Nope. I'm sound asleep."

Pal heard Dan giggle. There were various little noises that accompanied their getting out of bed and dressing. Tail wagging happily, Pal met them at the foot of the stairs. He went first to Jeff, who gave him a pat on

the head, then he offered his morning greeting to Dan. These ceremonies complete, he padded over to stand in front of the door. Jeff understood.

"I'll let you out."

Pal slipped through the opened door and waited for a while in front of the cabin. This was his country, but he had not forgotten that it had rejected him. He had walked safely with Johnny Blazer, but he had been clubbed and stoned after Johnny was no longer with him. The lesson had penetrated deeply.

When Pal finally left the cabin, he did not go down the path but went at once into the brush and walked slowly. Alone, he had better be careful. He

stopped when he caught the scent of a rabbit that was hiding in the brush. For a moment he was tempted to chase it because chasing rabbits was fun. But this morning he had a more urgent mission. Still walking slowly, nose questing and ears alert, he made his way to the road and halted in some thick brush beside it. He would not expose himself on the open road until he knew what lay ahead.

Across the road, and up the opposite slope, a doe and fawn were feeding. Pal caught the faint odor of grouse, and he knew that a skunk had wandered that way last night. Later, a fox had minced along.

The nearest human scents were those of Dan and Jeff, and as soon as he was sure of that, Pal considered himself safe. He ventured into and moved slowly down the road, but as he drew near the big sycamore he broke into an eager trot. It was at the sycamore that he had last seen Johnny Blazer, and there that he had lost all trace of him. Now he wanted to find if there was anything he might have overlooked.

He had given up all hope of finding Johnny; his long search had convinced him that his former master would never be found. But not forgotten, never to be forgotten, was his long association with Johnny, his love for him, and the good life they had lived together. Pal was going to the sycamore for the same reason that a human being rereads old letters written by a dear companion whom he will never see again. Once more he stopped to read the wind currents and the tracks in the road. Besides the fox and skunk, only Jeff's scent remained right there. Therefore Jeff was the only human who had used the road last night. But Pal caught the fainter scents of Smithville and

45

the people inhabiting it. They were distant odors and no one was coming. He gave undivided attention to the sycamore.

Winds had blown and rains had fallen, but Johnny Blazer had bled here and his scent still lingered. Pal drank long and deeply of it. He made a little circle, as though the scent should lead him farther. But it ended at the tree, and the dog came back to sniff again. He moaned softly in his throat, because his affection for Johnny had been great. But Johnny's scent ended where it began, at the sycamore. About to cast again, Pal halted in his tracks.

The morning breeze blew directly from Smithville to him, and the breeze had told him that nobody was coming. Now that was changed. Clearly

Pal caught the scent of Pete Whitney and he knew that Pete was walking up the road. The dog bristled, but not because he saw any connection between Pete and Johnny's disappearance. He knew only that all Whitneys were enemies and that Pete had been near when Johnny was hurt.

He crouched in the brush, undecided for the moment. If he lay perfectly still, Pete probably would pass without seeing him. But as the man drew nearer, Pal's nervousness increased. He decided suddenly that he would be safer with Jeff.

Pete was just a short distance away when Pal cleared the road in one bound and raced toward the cabin. The dog knew that he had been seen, but he did not care. The one dangerous time had been the fleeting instant he'd needed to cross the road and that was dangerous only because the road offered no cover. Once in the brush, he could run away from any man.

He found Dan drawing water from the spring beside the cabin and slowed to a walk. Because he had run hard, he was panting. He paused very close to the boy and looked nervously back toward the road. Dan stared curiously at him.

"What's down there?" he questioned. "What'd you find, Pal?"

The great dog turned toward Dan and wagged his tail as evidence of good will. But his hackles remained raised as he accompanied the boy into the cabin. The good smell of frying bacon perfumed the air. Standing over the stove, Jeff looked around questioningly.

"Isn't that bucket a load for you, Dan?" "Nah! I can carry it."

Jeff grinned. Most boys were proud of their physical prowess and he had not offended Dan by offering to draw the water for him. He broke eggs into the sputtering skillet. Pal growled and Jeff turned again to look.

"What's ailing him?"

"I don't know. He must have smelled something he don't like. When he came up to me, he was running."

Pal, knowing that Pete Whitney was coming toward the cabin, retreated to the far end of the room and stood. Still bristling, he showed his teeth. Jeff was puzzled.

"What's the-?"

"Something's around," Dan said quickly. He looked out of the window. "Jeff! Pete Whitney's coming!"

Eyes blazing, he looked toward the shotgun. Jeff saw and interpreted his glance.

"Remember! We're not going off half-cocked." "Uh-All right."

Jeff opened the door and saw the man standing in front of the cabin. Pete Whitney's clothing was slipshod, but that alone did not give him the air he

had. Jeff was not able to place it at once. There was something about him that should not be, something very like a surly animal. About thirty, Pete had fine blond hair that seemed rooted so precariously that the slightest wind might blow it away. His unshaven cheeks were covered with stubble.

Pale blue eyes shifted sideways, and he raised a foot as though about to run. Yet, at the same time, it was as though he had no intention of running. As far as Jeff could see, he carried no firearms, but he acted as though he were armed, and doubtless he was. Mentally, Jeff compared him to the man he had met yesterday. That man had also been careless of his clothing and appearance, but there was a strength and character in his being that was not evident in Pete. Barr Whitney was strong. Pete was weak.

Jeff asked pleasantly, "Something I can do for you?"

"Nao." Pete spoke with a high nasal twang. "You live here?" "Since yesterday," Jeff said. "Dan and I are here together." "I swan!" Pete ejaculated. "I swan!"

Jeff saw that he was obviously frightened. In spite of the fact that he seemed to be a man who would take fright easily, he might need help.

"Are you in trouble?"

"Nao. It's jest that I was passin' up the raoad an'-an'-" He blurted out. "I swan I saw Johnny Blazer's big dog!"

Jeff thought swiftly. Why should seeing Johnny Blazer's dog be cause for such alarm? He asked casually, "Where'd you see him?"

"Down thar on the raoad! I swan-a ha'nt dog!"

Jeff understood and relaxed. Many of the mountain people believed firmly in haunts, spirits and witchcraft. And everybody around Smithville had reason to believe that Pal must be dead. With an effort, Jeff concealed his amusement. A man such as this, thinking Johnny Blazer's dog dead and coming suddenly upon him, might tremble easily.

"You did see him," Jeff said. "He's here." "He be?"

For a split second, Pete's eyes lost their lack-luster appearance and venom flooded them. A cold finger brushed Jeff's spine. Any man able to look like that was a dangerous one. Jeff thought of his pack and of the shotgun in its corner. Then he decided that he could handle Pete, and meanwhile there were the amenities to be observed.

"Had breakfast?" "Nao."

"Come on in and have some."

Pete shuffled into the cabin. Mouth taut and eyes angry, Dan backed toward Pal. The dog growled savagely. Jeff's eyes caught Dan's and he tried to flash a warning. He and Dan had a pact which included no hasty or ill-timed moves and definitely no shooting of anyone. Jeff spoke sharply to the dog.

"Stop it, Pal!"

Pal subsided and Pete said nasally, "Blazer allus call't him Buster." "He's Pal now."

Jeff set a plate of bacon and eggs on the table and put bread and butter beside it. "You may as well start, Dan."

Unable completely to erase the anger from his eyes, not speaking, Dan sat down and began to eat. Jeff put the bacon and eggs he had intended for himself on another plate. Thoughtfully he set the plate on the other side of the table, two places away from the furious Dan.

"Here you are, Mr.-?"

"Whitney's the name. Pete Whitney." "I'm Jeff Tarrant and this is Dan Blazer."

"Yeah?" Interest leaped in Pete's eyes. "Any kin to John?" "He was my pop!" Dan flared. "That you know very well!"

"Dan, mind your manners!" Jeff remonstrated, putting more bacon and eggs in the skillet.

"I'm minding them! He knows who my pop was and he knows me!"

Pete, who had been eating as though finishing the meal was a job he had to complete in a great hurry, put his fork down and bent over his plate. Again Jeff thought uncomfortably of a hunted animal, and though he could not see Pete's eyes, he was sure that they were once more venom-ridden. There was an awkward silence which Pete broke.

"Seems to me I do mind a young'un comin' to see John."

Dan flared again. "Do you also 'mind' that my pop was shot? Maybe you even know who shot him!"

"Dan!" Jeff thundered.

For a few seconds Pete lingered over his food. Then it was as though he had thought out a decision which had been hard to make. He speared half an egg, curled a whole strip of bacon on the end of his fork, shoved everything into his mouth and began to chew noisily.

"Nao," he said. "I wouldn't knaow who done fer John."

"Dan's upset," Jeff explained. "He didn't realize what he was saying."

An explosive, "I did, too" lingered on Dan's lips and died there when he caught Jeff's eyes. As the latter turned to lift his own breakfast out of the skillet, Pete nodded vigorously.

"Likely. Likely. Young'uns do get upsot. What be ye doin' here?"

Jeff said smoothly, "We represent Tarrant Enterprises, Ltd., and came because we thought we could do some business around Smithville."

Pete's shifty eyes found Jeff's pack. "Peddler, huh?" "Some people call it that."

"Whar'd ye find the dog?"

"Over beyond Cressman. He made himself at home with us."

Jeff put his own plate on the table and began to eat. Pete mopped up the last of his breakfast with a crust of bread, plopped it into his mouth, and licked his fingers. That done, he picked up the conversation where it had been dropped.

"Take care he ain't kil't." "Take care who isn't killed?"

"The dog. He turned right snarly after Blazer was kil't. Bill Ellis'd a shot him if he hadn't took a mind to run away."

"Did he hurt anybody?" "Nao. But he had a mind to."

48

Pete leaned back, looking at the ceiling and cleaning his teeth with his tongue. He asked suddenly, "Whar'd ye get the young'un?"

For a moment Jeff fumbled. But Tarrant Enterprises, Ltd., had taught him that it was not a good idea to be at a loss long enough to let anyone else think too far ahead of him. He said glibly, "Dan was farmed out to me."

Jeff referred to the common practice of placing with accredited people who would support them, youngsters who had no other place to turn. Dan glared. Jeff did not look at him.

Pete Whitney said, "You git a smart lot of work out'en a farmed-out young'un if you whomp him to it."

Jeff's next words erased Dan's glare. "Dan doesn't need 'whomping.' We're full partners."

"Aoh."

There was another silence. Finally Pete Whitney asked, "What ye peddlin?"

"What do you need?" "I ast you."

"Cash or swap?"

"Swap." Pete looked surprised that anyone should think he had cash. "What can you swap?"

Pete reached inside his shirt and drew out a knife. It was much cruder than the works of art Jeff had had from Bart Whitney. But it was sturdy, and the blade, Jeff thought wryly, was certainly keen enough to penetrate anything that Pete might have reason to stab. Since there was a buyer for everything, it stood to reason that there would be a buyer for Pete's knife. Jeff went to his pack, took out a cheap jackknife, a compass and a wrapped parcel. He extended the knife.

"I'll swap even for this."

Pete accepted the knife, opened it, tried the blade on the back of his horny hand, and passed it back.

"Nao. That piddlin' thin'd bend on rabbit fur."

Enjoying himself, as he always did when bartering, Jeff handed the compass over. Pete looked at it. Puzzled, he glanced back at Jeff.

"Do it tell the hour?"

Dan laughed. Jeff explained. "It's called a compass. See? The needle always points north. Anyone who carries this can tell any direction at all."

Pete was honestly astounded. "You mean they's some what cain't?" "There are some, but I thought you wouldn't be one of them!"

He spoke admiringly, stressing the "you." Sales resistance faded to nothing if the seller, while convincing the buyer that he was much to be admired, could at the same time build up the buyer's opinion of himself. Like a good showman, Jeff had saved his masterpiece for last. He unwrapped the parcel to reveal a cheap box whose exterior was stamped with gaudy green dragons. Pete regarded it with narrowed eyes.

"This," Jeff said smoothly, "I offer to very few customers. Now if you'll just keep your eye on the box-"

Pete obliged, bending so closely that his face was no more than six inches from the box. Jeff pressed a button. The lid flew open and a green bellows surmounted by a grinning clown's head sprang up to hit Pete on the nose. He leaped backward, flung himself from the table and crouched. Again Jeff thought of an animal. But this time it was a beast of prey. And it was ready to strike.

The jack that had leaped out of the box quivered on the table, swaying this way and that. Completely astounded, Pete regarded it for a moment. Then sheer delight flooded his eyes.

"I swan!"

Jeff said proudly, "Ever see anything like that?" "Put it back!"

Jeff pressed the jack into place. Uncertainly, still a little fearful of such magic, Pete came near. He extended a hand and immediately withdrew it.

"Do it ag'in!"

Jeff pressed the button and the performance was repeated. Sure now that there was nothing to fear, Pete picked the toy up and looked at it closely. He pushed the jack down, latched the cover, and pressed the button. When the clown's head flew up, he tittered nervously.

"I swan!"

"For that I must have two knives." "Got but one."

Jeff frowned. The jack-in-the-box was a cheap trinket and the knife was worth four times as much. But Pete considered the jack a very valuable object and Jeff hoped to do much trading around Smithville. He did not want to be known for accepting the first thing offered and, besides, that was bad business. It took all the sport out of trading.

"Have to have something to boot," he said firmly. "I got this."

From his sagging pocket Pete took a length of braided horsehide. But it had been so skillfully cured and so expertly braided that it was strong as rope and pliable as the finest cloth. It would make a wonderful bridle rein, but Jeff said hesitantly, "I don't know what I'd use it for."

"Fer tyin' things."

"Well-" Jeff allowed himself to be convinced.

Pete sprung the jack again and again, fascinated by this simple thing which smacked of magic, because never before had he seen anything like it. Then, holding his jack-in-the-box as though it were eggshells, he made the swift transformation from fascinated child to dangerous man.

"Stick to peddlin'," he said shortly, and took his leave.

It was at the same time a threat and a warning and Jeff knew it. For a moment he sat still, then got up and strolled quietly to the window. Going down the path, Pete Whitney sprung the jack and his tittering giggle seemed again to be heard in the room.

7. GRANNY

Absorbed in watching Pete, Jeff was almost unaware when Dan came to stand beside him. As Pete disappeared, hidden by foliage, he turned away from the window and came face to face with Dan.

The boy's cheeks were flushed and hot anger burned in his eyes. Both fists were clenched so tightly that straining knuckles showed white.

Jeff said quietly, "Come out of it, Dan." "He's a Whitney!"

"Sorry you didn't shoot him?"

"I-It's not that, Jeff. I wasn't thinking very straight when I told you I aimed to shoot all the Whitneys. It's-Why should a Whitney be in my pop's cabin?"

"He was at our door and he was hungry." "Well-Doggonit, Jeff! You talk sense!"

Jeff heaved an inward sigh of relief. Yesterday Dan had not only talked of killing every Whitney, but he had acted fully capable of doing it. But yesterday he had been tired, hungry and so terribly alone. Good food and proper rest had worked a change, but they had not made him forget why he was here. Nothing would ever do that.

Dan asked, "You think we will get him, don't you?" "Get who?"

"Whoever killed my pop!"

"Murder can't be hidden, Dan," Jeff spoke with quiet forcefulness, "if somebody really wants to find it out."

"And we'll find out?" "We'll find out."

"Then," Dan gritted his teeth, "we'll shoot!"

Jeff said nothing. Dan was too young, too angry, and too steeped in the traditions of the hills, to think of anything except violent vengeance. Rather than tell him he was wrong, Jeff hoped to prove it. When they found whoever had murdered Johnny Blazer-and they must find him if Dan's tangled path was ever to be straight again-the law could take over. Jeff hoped that, at the right time, Dan would see such a course as the proper one. For the present, the less said the better.

"Let's get the place cleaned up and go out trading," Jeff suggested. "Good!"

Jeff washed dishes while Dan swept the floor, and it made no difference that it had also been swept last night. Only those with little regard for themselves were contented to accept dirty surroundings, and one way to keep dirt from accumulating was to clean often. The cabin in order, Jeff showed Dan his pack.

Each of its numerous straps, so adjusted that they opened at the flick of a finger, gave access to one compartment, and within themselves some of the compartments were further divided. They were also of various sizes. Obviously it was possible to carry a vast number of pins, needles, spools of thread, etc., in a somewhat small

51

space. Kitchen ware, of which Jeff had a considerable store, naturally needed more room. There was a place for bright ribbons, one for candy, and articles such as spices and tea were stored by themselves. Jeff had razor blades, pencils, an assortment of novelties such as the jack-in-the-box, a variety of small tools, nails, and both wood and metal screws. At the rear, reached by thrusting the hand through a hidden flap, were six more knives like the one he'd traded to Barr Whitney, meerschaum pipes, pocket watches, and a few other valuables that were best kept where they were not at once available or easily found.

Jeff explained that he always planned to carry as great an assortment as possible, with very few large articles. The partial bolt of gingham, the biggest single thing in the pack, he carried, not because there was much profit in carrying it, but because being able to offer gingham often provided an opening wedge to other sales. When he started, he had operated on a strictly cash basis

and had earned a fair amount of money doing so. Then he had discovered a great truth which had its foundations in the complexities of human nature. No matter what the article, from aardvark whiskers to zebra tails, somewhere somebody not only wanted it but wanted it badly enough to pay well. On the Atlantic Coast, Jeff had picked up a box of sea shells. In Indiana, he had met a trapper who'd never seen any sea shells and traded them for a bundle of mink pelts. Taking the pelts to Chicago, he had sold them to a furrier for more money than he might have earned in two weeks peddling for cash.

Though everything was precious, or at least desirable, to somebody, whoever had an abundance of any kind of goods was seldom inclined to regard it highly. But though they'd always sell for cash, whoever offered something that they wanted, did not have and would find it difficult to get, invariably made a better bargain. Jeff cited the knife and thong he had acquired from Pete Whitney. The jack-in-the-box had cost fifteen cents, but Jeff would be able to sell the knife for at least a dollar and twenty cents, and he did not know how much the horsehide thong would bring. But because Pete thought the jack-in- the-box such a treasure, and never would have been able to get one for himself, he hadn't been cheated.

Jeff concluded with the observation that peddlers had to recognize true value when they saw it. Otherwise they would not be able to remain in business.

Dan's eyes sparkled. "That sounds like fun!" "It has its points," Jeff admitted.

"Take me in with you for good!" Dan pleaded. "I want to be a peddler, too!"

Jeff glanced aside. He had taken this waif under his wing and could not abandon him. Then he was struck by the happy thought that Dan's request gave him control over his charge. "We'll see," he evaded the issue.

"Take me! I'll do anything if you'll teach me!" Jeff asked quickly, "Can I count on that?" "Anything! Just ask me!"

"You'll do exactly as I say?"

"Try it! What do you want done?"

Jeff grinned. "Right now let's go peddling-and leave the shotgun here."
"But-"

"You said you'd do anything." "Let's go, Jeff."

With an ease born of long experience, Jeff slipped into the pack.

Knowing that they were going out, Pal leaped to his feet and a doggy grin framed his jaws. Jeff closed the door but did not lock it. The cabin had been rifled only because it was thought abandoned. Known to be occupied, it was safe. The hill men might use force to get what they wanted, or even kill another man for it, but petty pilfering was beneath them.

The sun was warm without being too warm, and a breeze fanned the cheeks of the pair of peddlers. The smile was complete on Jeff's face, and laughter was in his heart. The horizon stretched limitlessly, with no end or definition, and good fortune was a certainty. He couldn't be other than happy.

"Where we going, Jeff?" Dan asked.

"I don't know. Let's follow our noses and go where they lead."

Jeff took the first mule and footpath that branched from the road, for he was sure that most of the people he wanted to see would be back in. Most hill people preferred plenty of room and they did not, as one hillbilly had expressed it to Jeff, like to be "All cluttered up with people. Skassly a week passes but what three, four go by."

Ranging ahead, Pal flushed a buck from its thicket, chased it a little way, and let it go. He returned to Jeff and Dan, lingered to sniff at some interesting rabbit tracks, and ran to catch up. There came a faint smell of wood smoke.

Jeff sniffed eagerly, trying to determine the smoke's origin, and he thought with some amusement that he was doing exactly as he had told Dan they would do. In a very real sense he was following his nose, and when he came to a less-traveled path that swung from the one they were following, he took it.

Pal at his heels, Dan bringing up the rear, he walked fast. In three minutes they came to a clearing. Apparently without plan, it had been hacked out of the forest. It was irregularly-shaped, probably to follow the easiest cutting, and a few large trees had been allowed to stand in it. There were many stumps, a small garden, a mule that hung its head over the topmost of two strands of rusting wire and looked cynical, and four half-wild pigs that squealed and scuttled into the brush. The barn, that had listed badly and seemed in immediate danger of falling, was propped up with saplings. The house, made of hand-hewn timbers, was very small and very old. Rains, snow, sun and wind had so beaten it that it had achieved a unique color all its own and somehow it looked sad.

Jeff knocked confidently and waited. The door opened an inch, then another inch, and in the gloomy interior Jeff saw, not too well, a scowling face that was framed in a veritable haystack of black hair and beard. But he saw very clearly the sinister snout of a rifle that was aimed squarely at his middle and he heard very clearly a growled,

"Git goin' an' start now!" "Right away," Jeff agreed.

He whirled and started back to the main path. Too over-awed to speak, Dan trotted at his heels and he dared say nothing until they were once more where they had started from. Then,

"Gee!" he breathed. "Weren't you scared?"

53

"No," Jeff answered wryly, "my heart always pounds." "Do you think he didn't want us around?"

"I had a slight suspicion." "What do we do now?"

"Find somebody else," Jeff said cheerfully. "It's part of peddling."

The day was too fine, and too sparkling, to be ruined by any surly mountaineer. They walked on, feet winged and hearts gay. Jeff thought whimsically that the money he made selling or trading was the very smallest part of the reward he received. By far the major portion lay in walks just like this, in the fact that he loved the work he was doing, and in trying to anticipate what lay ahead. He always tried to build up a mental picture of his next customer, always failed to do so, and invariably had to discard his carefully- rehearsed approach to create a new one on the spur of the moment. Much of the time he knew the sort of house in which his next prospect would live, but

nothing in his experience had prepared him for the house they found not a mile from the one they had left.

Rounding a bend, they saw a little hill. There was nothing majestic or imposing about it, for it was a very small hill. But it was a very beautiful one. It was as though the Creator of the mountains, after much deliberation, had decided that the little hill would fit nowhere except exactly where it was.

All the trees save one had been stripped from the side, Jeff and Dan could see, and the grass growing there was so green and soft that it was almost unreal. The one tree gave it just the right touch, so it was as though this hill were something out of fairyland. A little herd of sheep cropped the grass. Delighted, Jeff let his gaze stray upward.

"Gee but it's pretty!" Dan breathed.

"It is that," Jeff agreed. "Look at the house."

There were trees on the very top of the hill. Silhouetted against the blue sky, they seemed to be outlined against a gentle sea. A log house nestled in the grove. Something-at first Jeff thought it must be the whitewash that outlined all the windows and then he knew it was not-set the house apart. Like the hill, it was a fairyland house and Jeff knew that they must visit there.

The hill rose in undulating waves, with no harsh angles or uncouth lines to mar it. But it was not a park-like perfection. Some person, or persons, must have expended enormous labor to make the hill look as it did. But every line, every patch of grass, seemed to belong naturally just where it was.

Jeff could decide only that this was a happy hill and that whoever lived in the house was either the owner of a rare talent or blessed beyond belief by the angels. Or perhaps some of both.

They came to the house and marveled. It was made of logs and chinked with clay, but nothing haphazard had gone into its making. Even the chinking was not just slapped on and troweled in, but flowed in graceful lines as though it had always been part of the logs. As old as the cabin they had left, the house had a sheen instead of a sad and aged appearance. Whoever lived here must love it greatly.

"Howdy, boys."

The woman came around the house so silently and so unexpectedly that for a moment Jeff was startled. The top of her head reached scarcely to his shoulder. Her silver hair glowed like a halo, but there was something which was far from angelic in the remarkable eyes that dominated her unusual face. She wore a simple blue dress. Highlighted in silver, an exquisitely-stitched blue- bird in flight adorned the front of it. Her movements were quick and graceful. But there was no suggestion of frailty, and the muzzle loading rifle that swung easily from her right hand might have been a strong man's weapon.

Without any hesitation, Pal went forward to receive her caress. In a sudden rush of feeling, Jeff forgot his amazement and felt entirely at home. He knew all at once that everything and everybody was welcome on this hill.

"And howdy to you, Granny!" he said graciously. "I'm-" Jeff thought of introducing himself as Tarrant Enterprises, Ltd., but did not. "I'm Jeff Tarrant and this is Dan Blazer."

Her head flitted like a bird's. "And I'm Granny Wilson." "Wilson?" Jeff remembered. "I met an Ike Wilson in Cressman." "Did you now? Ike's one of my boys. What was he doin'?"

"He was-" Jeff fumbled. "Darned if I haven't forgotten!"

Her laugh was like rippling water. "He was in jail for stealin' chickens. You can say it, Jeff. It takes all kinds to make a family. My Tommy's a doctor, my Joel's a lawyer, my Billy's a sailor-" She named four more sons, all of whom were in some useful occupation, and finished, "They all followed their natural bent and Ike just naturally took to chicken stealin'." She turned to Dan. "You kin to Johnny Blazer?"

Dan said bashfully, "He was my pop."

"Come in," she invited. "Come in and set down to gingerbread and milk. I vow I've missed Johnny and I'm glad to have his kin! You come, too, Jeff, and fetch your dog!"

Jeff looked at the rifle. "Have you been hunting?"

"Land no!" She laughed. "I was shootin' at Brant Severance!" "You-!"

"Didn't hit him," she said. "Didn't aim to hit him. Just wanted to show him he couldn't pester my sheep."

"But-isn't there-"

She anticipated and forestalled his question. "Nope, I'm all alone. My boys, they want me to come with them. Land! I'd grow old and shrively in a city! Two houses are one too many! Do come in."

Granny opened the door that was made of carefully-mortised, hand- polished boards and adorned with an excellent wood carving that depicted a running buck chased by wolves. Jeff and Dan breathed their delight.

Except for the stove, the pots and pans that hung behind it, the lamps, and a few other articles that would be very difficult to fashion with hand tools, every bit of furniture had been made of whatever materials were available. But whoever made it had not been contented with something merely useful. Strict utility had received consideration, but beauty was in vast abundance.

Jeff looked through a large window that faced the back and saw a neat garden, a little grove of fruit trees, a fat mule, a brown cow, and a cat sitting on a stone. It was exactly the big, fluffy, white cat that should have belonged in such a place. Not until he took a second glance did he realize that the cat was not alive at all, but woven into a tapestry. He went nearer.

Stretched on a walnut frame, the tapestry was so exquisitely woven that the cat's every hair not only showed but was in the right place. The cat was about to lick a front paw, and even after he knew it was a tapestry, so real was the illusion of life that Jeff extended a hand to see if the cat might not be soft and warm. He turned to Granny.

"Who did this?"

She was all gentleness. "I did. That's my Kitty Cat, dead these four months."

There was longing in her voice, and more than a hint of sadness, and Jeff knew that the cat had meant a great deal to her. He understood. Some people loved horses, some preferred dogs, and some set their affections on cats. But for Granny it could not be just any cat.

Jeff asked, "Do you do much of this sort of thing?" "Land, yes! A body ought to keep busy!"

Jeff said gently, "I think you've kept busy a long while around here." "Sixty-four years the seventh of May," she said pertly. "Came as a

sixteen-year-old bride. Enos, God rest his soul, has been gone these past three years. You two come on into the kitchen."

She led them into the kitchen, seated them, opened a trap door in the floor, took cool milk from an earth-bound chamber, and lifted a tray of gingerbread from a cabinet. Eighty years old, her movements were almost as brisk and sure as a girl's. Jeff and Dan ate heartily; any food they prepared for themselves could not possibly compare with this. Granny seated herself companionably near.

"Ike say when he was gettin' out?" she asked.

"Well, no. He was there with Bucky-" Jeff snapped his fingers. "I forgot his last name."

"Bucky Edwards," she furnished. "Land! He and Ike been stealin' chickens for a span of time."

Jeff sensed something completely fine. She was old in years only. Until the day she died her mind would be young and strong. Ike's escapades probably did hurt her, but Ike was as much her son as the doctor, the lawyer and the others who had decided in favor of respectable careers. She would not deny him.

Jeff said, "Ike and Bucky didn't seem to have any definite plans." "They have some," she assured him. "They'll come here, and when they do, there'll be a heap of trouble-" She stopped suddenly, as though she had said something unwise.

"When do you expect them?" Jeff asked.

"Don't rightly know. Maybe soon. Maybe not so soon."

For a moment Jeff was silent and Dan was still stuffing gingerbread into his mouth. Granny had spoken of trouble when Ike came, but apparently it

was not trouble for herself, and if she wanted him to know more about it she would have told him. He wished he could offer her help, but he had an uncomfortable feeling that she knew how to help herself. He was trying to think of a way to steer the conversation away from Ike when Granny relieved him of the necessity for so doing.

"What you peddlin'?" she asked brightly.

Jeff fidgeted. The contents of his pack, for the most part, were designed for those who had little. Jeff tried to please people who yearned after a bit of gay ribbon, a new knife, anything they might need or desire but could not get for themselves. But he couldn't imagine what Granny lacked and countered her question with one of his own.

"Where do you get your thread and yarn?"

She looked surprised. "Spin it myself, to be sure. I have sheep. I grow flax, too."

Jeff followed up because he was interested. "Do you also make your own dyes?"

"Land, yes! 'Twould be a sin to let the yarbs go to waste when they grow right at the door step!"

"Do you use anything besides herbs?"

"Bark, seeds, nut husks and shells, it's all here. Take a bit of this, a bit of that, a bit of another thing, seethe it, and there's a dye."

"I know you do your own weaving." "Land, yes!"

Jeff grinned ruefully. For the first time since its founding, Tarrant Enterprises, Ltd., had reached a blind end. "Something for Everyone," was one of its numerous slogans. But he did not have anything for Granny Wilson and he was honest about it.

"Granny, I don't believe I can offer you a thing." "Oh, come now! You must have somethin'!" "But I haven't."

"Now, Jeff, you jest open that pack and give me a look for myself." "I'll do that much."

Jeff laid his pack on the table and opened every compartment. Granny reached for a skein of gray yarn. She tested it with her fingers, murmured, "Poorly, poorly," and handed it back. Granny ignored the bright ribbons, had no time whatever for the knickknacks, lingered over a packet of needles, and her eyes were accusing when she gave them back.

"Young man, you are a poor shakes of a peddler." "I tried to tell you I hadn't anything you'd want."

"You should have somethin' to please a poor old woman."

"I know. If I had anything good enough for you-Oh, darn!"

A skein of yarn tumbled out of the pack and caught on a buckle. Jeff reached through the slit for one of the many-bladed knives, opened the scissors, and carefully snipped the tangled wool off. Granny clapped joyful hands.

"I knew it! I knew it! Give me that."

Jeff handed her the knife. Granny's eyes shone.

"Just the thing!" she cried ecstatically. "Just what I need! My eyes ain't what they used to be. I missed two shots at runnin' bucks last fall and I'm forever mislayin' my necessaries. 'Twould be handy to have so many in one piece. Cash or swap?"

Jeff said recklessly, "Let's call it a gift, Granny."

"But," she was honestly troubled, "you can't give me aught that cost you dear."

"Yes I can."

57

"Not by my leave," she said firmly. "It's only right that a body gets his worth."

"I'll swap even for a look at some of your other tapestries." "My what?"

"Your cloth pictures, like the cat." "Land! I'll get some."

She bounced from her chair, bustled into an adjoining room, and they heard her open a trunk. A moment later she was back with two tapestries under her arm. She spread one, a yard long by about twenty inches wide, and Jeff gasped.

It was The Last Supper, but instead of following conventional patterns, Granny had drawn inspiration from the life around her. Jesus and His disciples were seated at a wooden table that was innocent of any adornment or finery whatsoever, but the table was so finely done that a sliver thrusting out from it seemed both real and symbolic. There was an air of dignity that rose above mere human dignity, and the dyes had been applied with a touch so delicate that holy light seemed to emanate from the picture. Its message was one of hope. Judas was not to be abandoned.

"Do you like it?" Granny asked.

"It-" Jeff was at a loss for words. "It's wonderful!" "Preacher Skiles thinks the Lord ain't right."

"Preacher Skiles assumes a great deal of responsibility."

She laughed. "'Twas not the way he meant it. He thinks Jesus should be sittin' above the rest, with maybe angels flyin' at His shoulder."

"It's better this way."

"That's what I thought," Granny asserted. "The Lord, He wasn't above the beggars, the sick and those who done wrong. Somehow I got to think of Him as comin' down to all of us."

"I, too."

"This one," Granny spread the other tapestry, "I call The Fall of Satan." Jeff gasped again. The picture centered around the black silhouette of

Satan, with a background done in delicate shades of red. There was about the figure utter misery, abandonment and despair. The gates of hell, which he had not yet entered, were merely suggested. But they were suggested so artistically that one sensed the seething fires, the complete torment, that awaited.

Dan looked and shuddered. "Gee!"

Jeff breathed, "Why hasn't anyone else seen these, Granny?"

"Enos," she answered, "didn't hold with hangin' them on the walls and I've tried to keep the house as Enos'd want it. But I knew Enos wouldn't mind Kitty Cat. He-he's company."

"Somebody should see them."

"Pooh! Who'd bother with an old woman's foolishness?" "I would."

"Then take them. Take them for the knife." "I won't do it."

She seemed crestfallen. "I didn't think you would."

Jeff said seriously, "It isn't that. These are worth a great deal of money."

"They are? How much?"

Jeff hazarded a guess, "Twenty-five dollars." "Land!"

"Each," Jeff finished. "My land!"

"Granny, do you trust me?"

"Pooh! I didn't raise eight of my own 'thout knowin' aught of boys." "Are these dear to you?"

"I don't set much store by 'em. Enos never liked 'em."

"Let me take them into Ackerton," Jeff urged. "Let me see what I can do with them there."

"Go ahead if you've a mind to. Land! Meal time and I haven't started a thing for you boys to eat!"

8. ACKERTON

Jeff awakened an hour before sunrise. He raised himself on his bunk and listened. Dan's regular breathing proved that he still slept, and Jeff settled back beneath his warm blankets to do some thinking.

In some respects, the trading around Smithville had not gone as well as he had hoped it would. The hill men had been eager for his knives of many uses, his fishing tackle, his small tools, his nails and all the bolts and screws he had. They had also taken all the novelties. But they had spurned his inferior products because they could make better ones themselves, and Jeff had been able to trade only one watch. Watches were useless to those who guided themselves by the sun.

The women had been happy over the gay ribbons, the thread and yarn, the pins and needles, and the bolt of gingham had gone in two days. It was better and more colorful than anything Abel Tarkman stocked. But the women had wanted only a small portion of his kitchenware and spices. Jeff had traded all his cinnamon, pepper, tea and the few other things that could not be found locally. But no hill woman would think of offering anything at all for what she could find growing within easy reach of her doorstep or was able to produce in her garden.

The candy had been exhausted by the third day, and Jeff grinned at the way it had gone. He had conceived what he thought was the clever idea of bribing the children with it, and he had discovered that the older folks had a sweet tooth, too. Never to be forgotten was Grandpa Severance, sucking a striped peppermint stick with toothless jaws.

59

However, in other respects, trading had far exceeded Jeff's fondest hopes.

Though the hill people had rejected some of his wares, they had been willing to pay well for what they did want. Jeff and Dan had visited their cabins or met them on the trails, for news that a peddler who'd rather trade than sell was abroad had penetrated into the remotest valleys. Jeff had a dozen hunting knives whose quality ranged from fair to superb. There were three exquisitely balanced hand-made hatchets, a wonderfully polished hunting horn, a set of fine miniatures made of deer antler, a fringed buckskin shirt, four pairs of superior moccasins and other articles, including an ancient matchlock pistol still in working order. Granny Wilson's tapestries remained his biggest prize.

Jeff knew that, beyond any doubt, his week's work had paid him more than any previous month's. But he knew also that he would have to get trade

goods that conformed to the hill people's idea of what they wanted. Therefore, in order to get new stock and dispose of the wares he had, a trip to Ackerton was necessary. That presented a problem.

Dan had traveled with him all week. Far from lagging, his interest in trading had heightened. So far Dan had kept his promise and had done as Jeff said. But by the fastest route it would take a full day to go to Ackerton, a full day to return, and Jeff thought that he would need at least four or five days in the city. What would Dan do if Jeff were not there to restrain him? The boy had never forgotten that a blood feud had brought him back to Smithville.

Dan's bunk rustled and he whispered, "Jeff." "I'm here."

"Just wanted to see if you're awake."

As it usually did when he needed it most, happy inspiration came to Jeff.

"I'm awake all right and I want you to do something for me." "Sure, Jeff."

"I'm going to Ackerton today and I may be gone a week or more. I

want you to take Pal and go up to watch over Granny Wilson." "But-"

"She needs somebody," Jeff urged. "You and I have stopped in there almost every day and kept an eye on her. We can't just leave her alone."

Dan said reluctantly, "All right, Jeff. Can I take the shotgun?" "You'd just better."

His problem neatly solved, Jeff relaxed. When Dan announced that he had been assigned as her protector, Granny, in her wisdom, would accept him as such. If he should get out of hand, the shotgun shells were loaded with nothing but paper. They'd make a satisfactory noise but wouldn't hurt anybody.

Jeff prepared their breakfasts, they cleaned the cabin, and with the shotgun over one shoulder, half-pulling the unwilling Pal with his free hand, Dan started for Granny Wilson's. Pack on his shoulder, Jeff strode into Smithville.

There were two routes to Ackerton. The hard one was over the mountains. The easy one was eighteen miles down the logger's road to Delview, where a train could be boarded, and Jeff chose that way. He walked swiftly, anxious to make time, but even as he walked he filed in his mind the locations of the cabins he either passed or saw evidence of. There were vast possibilities for trade around Smithville. So far he and Dan had explored only a small part of it.

Half past twelve brought him to Delview, and Jeff walked openly down the street. Larger than Cressman, Delview was busier, and Jeff's peddling instincts cried for expression. He submerged them; a city was the only place to

offer the wares he carried now. Jeff stopped when a policeman tapped his shoulder.

"Are you peddling?"

"No," Jeff answered blandly, "just passing through." "You come from Cressman?"

"Cressman? I came from Smithville." "Just thought I'd ask. Been fishing?" "Hunting," Jeff said gravely.

He grinned to himself and walked on. Obviously, Pop and Joe Parker had sent word to Delview, but just as obviously they'd told the police there to be alert for a red-headed peddler accompanied by a huge dog. On impulse, Jeff stopped at a drugstore, bought a postcard, addressed it to Joe Parker, and wrote, "Thanks for sending me to Delview. Regards to Pop. Happy days."

He signed it J. Seymour Tarrant, Esq., dropped it into a mail box, made his way to the station and bought a ticket to Ackerton.

Leaving Delview at half past three, and stopping several times en route, the train did not reach Ackerton until a quarter to eight. Jeff bore the slow ride serenely, for only the unwise thought that they must forever hurry. Besides, time could always be used to good advantage and the slow train was a heaven- sent opportunity to work out a plan. Arriving in Ackerton, Jeff had a clear idea of just what he wanted to do there.

He left the train and made a confident way through the huge station. He had the pack on his back because that was the easiest way to carry it, and he met the curious stares directed at him with a good-natured grin. He was as out of place here as a well-dressed Ackertonite would have been in Smithville, and he elicited the same curiosity. But he did not mind because he had been in cities before and he would be forgotten as soon as he was out of sight. Jeff's questing eyes found a paper banner displayed above one of the station's newsstands:

HOTEL KENNARD, ACKERTON'S BEST

He glanced at the banner and followed a pointing arrow with TAXI stenciled on it. Imperiously he beckoned the lead cab and directed, "The Hotel Kennard."

The cabbie looked questioningly at him. "The Kennard?"

"The Kennard," Jeff repeated, "and since I know the shortest way, you might as well follow it."

The cabbie shrugged; if this ill-dressed traveler wanted to go to the Kennard, and was able to pay for the trip, that was his affair. Jeff relaxed in the back seat and gave himself over to enjoying a city's sights, sounds, and bustle. Maybe, if he were a very wealthy merchant, instead of a peddler, he would enjoy such a place himself. A moment later he decided that he wouldn't. Half his fun lay in personal contact with customers, and there was little that was

personal about city business. The cab halted at the curb and the driver opened the door.

"Just a second," Jeff directed.

61

He glanced swiftly at the Kennard and was satisfied. It was in one of the better sections, and the well-dressed men and women going in and out were proof enough that it was, if not the best, at least one of the best hotels. Thus Jeff had the base of operations that he wanted. He paid the cabbie and entered the hotel.

The lobby was plush, with thick carpeting, marble pillars, and the usual quota of those who were waiting or simply loafing in upholstered chairs. Heads rose, and Jeff winked slyly at an obviously affluent man who peered at him over the top of a paper. Embarrassed, the man ducked back beneath his paper. Jeff made his way to the desk.

"First floor room with bath," he directed loftily. "I wish to be away from street noises and," he looked critically around the lobby, "I prefer the better furnishings."

The blase clerk, who had registered all sorts of guests but few like this, took Jeff's measure with his eye.

"Those rooms are five dollars a day."

"My good man! I asked for a room, not advice!"

"Ye-" the clerk was still suspicious but he was also there to rent rooms. "Yes, sir. Overnight only?"

"My stay is indefinite."

Jeff signed the register with a flourishing "Jeffrey S. Tarrant," accepted the key and gave his pack over to a solemn-faced bellboy who led him down a corridor. He examined the room as he entered, displayed a dollar bill, flipped a quarter and said to the bellboy,

"Bring me a city directory, will you?" "Yes, sir."

The bellboy left, knocked discreetly a few minutes later, handed Jeff a bulky directory, and Jeff tipped him a dollar. He washed and, careless of the glances he attracted, enjoyed a good dinner in the Kennard's dining room. Then he returned to his room, belly-flopped on the bed, opened the directory, laid a pencil and sheet of paper on it and began to run his finger down the columns. He came to "Barnerson, Joseph D., dlr. antqes. 413 Grand Ave.," and wrote the information on his sheet of paper. Jeff noted five more dealers in antiques, six sporting goods stores and six shops chosen at random which, from their listings, seemed to cater to exclusive trade. That done, he referred to a city map in the same book and drew a line through whatever did not seem to be in one of Ackerton's better districts.

The first phase of his campaign was outlined. Jeff rang for the evening papers and read until he was too sleepy to read any more.

From force of habit he awoke at dawn, but turned over and went back to sleep. The hill people began their day with the first light, but he was in a city now. Jeff awoke again at eight o'clock, breakfasted and made his way to the street. He wandered down it and entered the first clothing store he found.

"I want a business suit," he told the clerk who accosted him. "This way, sir."

The clerk tried to read Jeff, thought he'd succeeded, and brought out a suit that had been in style fifteen years ago and probably in storage since.

Jeff rose with a curt, "Don't you have any new suits?" "Oh! Sorry, sir. My error."

He fitted Jeff with a neat blue serge suit, a white shirt, a modest but smart tie, a pair of socks, and new shoes. Jeff took his old clothes back to the Kennard, wrapped one of Barr Whitney's knives, thrust it into his inside coat pocket and went out. His trap was set and scented. Now he had to see if he would catch anything.

There were four sporting goods stores still on his list, but Jeff passed the first because its windows were dirty and the second because it advertised a bargain sale. But the third seemed to offer what he wanted. He asked the friendly clerk who came forward, "Is Mr. Ryerson in?"

"No, he isn't. But Mr. Calworth is." "May I see him?"

"This way."

Jeff followed the clerk down the aisle and examined the store closely as he did so. The fire arms, fishing tackle and other sporting equipment displayed on the counters was all of quality make and he hadn't been asked for an appointment, so evidently this store catered to sportsmen able to afford the best and at the same time it was not overly formal. The clerk ushered him into an office and Jeff's hopes rose.

"Mr. Calworth," the clerk said, "this gentleman wants to see you."

"My name's Tarrant," Jeff shook Mr. Calworth's extended hand, "Jeff Tarrant, and I'd hoped you'd be kind enough to furnish me with some information."

"Sit down, Mr. Tarrant."

Mr. Calworth was middle-aged, and a sprinkling of gray showed in his black hair. But there was a sparkle in his eyes, an ease of movement and callouses on his hands. Obviously he did something besides sit at a desk, and Jeff guessed shrewdly that he was an outdoor enthusiast himself. Jeff took the proffered chair and draped himself carelessly, but not too carelessly, upon it.

"I represent Tarrant Enterprises," Jeff almost added the Ltd., but caught himself in time. "We may wish to expand."

"Are you in sporting goods?" "Partly."

"And you're considering Ackerton?"

"Yes and no. That's what I hope to decide." "There's plenty of room, Mr. Tarrant." "But how much good room?"

Mr. Calworth laughed. "I'll tell you frankly. There are a variety of sporting goods stores, but Ryerson and Hapley split forty-five per cent of the trade and ninety per cent of the most desirable trade. However, there is no reason why an aggressive newcomer should not do very well."

Jeff bent forward. "Is there a survey-Oh!" Purposely arranged to do so, the knife in his pocket had slipped and thrust the front of his new coat outward. Grinning his embarrassment, Jeff took the knife from his pocket and balanced it on his knee.

Mr. Calworth's eyes followed his movements. "What do you have there?" piece."

"One of our specialties." Jeff gave him the knife. "A rather exceptional Mr. Calworth slipped the knife from its sheath, and his eyes warmed as

he examined it. He tested the blade with his thumb and shaved a couple of hairs from the back of his hand. When he turned to Jeff, he was interested.

"You specialize in this sort of thing?"

"We specialize in quality," Jeff said casually. "When we sell, we like to believe that the customer receives full value."

"Do you get many articles as good?"

Jeff shrugged. "Look at it. Can that be mass-produced?"

"No," Mr. Calworth admitted. "What is your retail price on this knife?" "Twenty dollars," Jeff said firmly.

"When do you intend to open your branch, Mr. Tarrant?"

"I'm not sure we will open it. At least, we won't until after much more extensive research."

"Would you care to make Ryerson your agent until you decide definitely?"

Jeff deliberated. Then, "I hadn't thought of an agency."

"It can't hurt you and it might make you some money. I'll continue to be frank. This is not something to offer an average customer because he simply cannot afford it. But there are sportsmen who can, and they come to Ryerson's. We'll take this, and any other quality merchandise you have, at a thirty per cent discount."

Jeff thought of Barr's other knife, a few of the rest, the hatchets, the bridle reins, and made a swift calculation. Not all were equally valuable, but all were quality. If Ryerson paid him cash, he would more than make up for everything he had dispensed from his pack, his train fare, his expenses in

Ackerton, and he would still have valuable goods. He said finally, "It should work to our mutual benefit."

"May we expect some more soon?" Mr. Calworth asked.

"I have a few in my sample case at the Kennard. You may have those as soon as I've time to deliver them and more in-shall we say three weeks?"

"I'll send a clerk for what you have," Mr. Calworth promised, "and leave your check at the Kennard desk. Or would you prefer payment to your business headquarters?"

Jeff held his breath inwardly, but answered quite casually, "It doesn't matter."

"We'll leave it at the Kennard," Mr. Calworth decided. "What should the total be?"

Jeff made a swift mental calculation. Barr Whitney's two knives for twenty dollars each, one almost as good for fifteen, two for ten and three for five dollars each. Pete's horsehide thong for four dollars and the three hatchets at five dollars each. That less thirty per cent. Jeff gave the total, "Seventy-six dollars and thirty cents."

"Good!" Jeff knew that this keen man would examine each article and see if the price was suitable. "Are you going back to the Kennard?"

"I must stop in for a few minutes."

"May I send someone along to pick up the rest of the things?" "Certainly."

"Fine! Don't forget us, Mr. Tarrant."

Jeff walked back to the Kennard with one of Ryerson's clerks, gave him the merchandise intended for him in the lobby and got a receipt. Then he returned to his room, looked over the motley collection of knives that remained, and decided that he could sell or trade them to his advantage. But he wanted to take care of some of the other articles first and then give special attention to Granny's tapestries. He examined the pistol and the set of miniatures. Both were unknown quantities.

About a foot long, the pistol had a metal barrel and ivory handles that had faded to a soft yellow. On each handle was an elaborate boar's head. Nat Stancer, who had traded Jeff the pistol for two screwdrivers, had kept it in good working order. Jeff did not know how much it was worth, but certainly it would be of use only to a hill man or to someone interested in antiques.

The miniatures were small but well carved and proportioned, and all of them consisted of deer in various stages and poses. There were a doe and fawn, a running buck, a lone fawn, three grazing does, a resting buck and a doe rearing. They had cost Jeff a yard each of red, blue and yellow ribbon, but the woman who had traded them had not done the carving. The miniatures were also old and Jeff thought they had probably been fashioned by some invalid with nothing else to do.

The pistol in one side pocket and the miniatures in another, Jeff set out to visit the antique dealers whose names and addresses he had listed. With no experience in antiques, he had only a vague idea as to how to go about sellin his, so he took the dealers in alphabetical order and the first name on his list was Joseph Barnerson.

He entered the store, a narrow building sandwiched between two larger ones, and looked curiously at the objects surrounding him. Jeff recognized few and wanted none, but looking at them strengthened his own conviction that, no matter what the article might be, it was desirable to somebody. Jeff turned toward the man who came to meet him. He had half expected somebody old and creaking, but this man was only about thirty and far from decrepit.

"What may I do for you?"

"I have an old pistol," Jeff said, "and maybe I'd sell it if I got the right price."

The man smiled. "Mister, I sell antiques. I do not buy them." "You don't? Where do you get your stock then?"

The smile became a grin. "I get my merchandise in my own way. Let me see your pistol."

Jeff handed it over. The man examined it closely and finally said, "They're a drug on the market. I'll give you fifty cents."

"In that case, wrap up six for me. I'll give you three dollars for 'em." "Where would I get six?"

"You said they're a drug on the market."

"So," the man admitted, "are most other antiques. Their value depends on how badly somebody wants them. Find somebody who wants the pistol and you'll get a fair price. To somebody who doesn't want it, it isn't worth a penny."

"That makes sense."

"What are you going to do now?" "Find somebody who wants it."

But, though Jeff visited other dealers in antiques, none offered him more than a dollar for the pistol and nobody offered anything for the miniatures. It was very late when he returned to the Kennard.

9. MIGHTY MISSION

In his room at the Kennard, Jeff slept late. The past four days had been busy ones, and more than a little hectic, and he was tired.

Mr. Calworth himself had brought back three of the cheapest knives. Admittedly they were worth five dollars each, but they were not merchandise that Ryerson could sell to its more exacting customers. If they were to pay premium prices, they demanded premium quality and Ryerson had better knives in stock that they sold for four dollars and a half. However, Mr. Calworth had softened their return by taking the fringed hunting shirt, the four pairs of moccasins and the polished hunting horn, and privately Jeff kicked himself for failing to offer them in the first place. They had brought thirty-eight dollars and Ryerson's would take all Jeff could supply if the quality remained as good.

The pistol was also gone. Failing to sell it to anyone at the price he wanted to get, Jeff had carelessly left it on his dresser. The maid who tidied up the room had found it, decided that only a desperate outlaw would use such a thing and taken to it the clerk. Unable to resolve a situation so grave, and unwilling to take the responsibility, the clerk had consulted the manager and the manager had come to see Jeff.

He apologized for his employees but thought that they had been well intentioned. He also recognized the pistol and it just so happened that his hobby was collecting antique fire arms. If Jeff cared to sell the pistol-Jeff did, for fifteen dollars.

Jeff had tramped the streets, going from store to store and bartering. It had taken time. But bit by bit he had rid himself of almost everything he had brought to Ackerton and stocked his pack with items the hill people favored. None of it had cost Jeff any money and, in addition to all expenses, he had a clear profit of almost a hundred dollars. Under ordinary circumstances that would have been excellent. But these circumstances were not ordinary.

He had been unable to find a buyer for either the miniatures or Granny Wilson's tapestries.

Though it revolted his peddler's instincts to do so, he was willing to keep the miniatures if it took too much time to sell them. Not only did he refuse to do so with Granny's tapestries, but he was determined to settle for nothing less than the price he

66

had assured Granny he could get. However, at least for the moment, he had reached a stalemate.

Jeff had visited every store that seemed to have a wealthy trade. But the most expensive tapestry he had been shown cost twelve dollars and fifty cents and he hadn't even bothered to show Granny's.

Jeff turned over, opened his eyes, sat up, yawned and occupied his mind with the problems of the day. The smile remained on his lips and his eyes retained their sparkle. The fact that he had had no success with the tapestries proved only that he had not yet offered them to the right person. They were a challenge, and it was a challenge to which he could rise. If he had permitted himself to be discouraged by every small setback, he would have stopped peddling long ago.

He dressed, breakfasted and lingered over his plate to ponder the problem of the tapestries. Naturally one did not walk up to any stranger, ask him if he needed an expensive tapestry and proceed to sell him one. But there had to be a way because there was always a way. What way? Jeff tried his best to come up with an answer and couldn't do it. He still had no intention of leaving Ackerton until the tapestries were sold.

Jeff fell back on the idea that first things must be first and he still had more to do in Ackerton. Maybe something would occur to him while he was doing it.

He went to his room, referred to the directory, found the Jackson School for Boys, noted its address on a slip of paper and tucked one of Granny's tapestries, The Last Supper, under his arm before he left the hotel. Far from doing so only once, Opportunity was always knocking, and Jeff thought that many people missed her visit only because they were unprepared when she was all but hammering the door from its hinges.

Jeff took a taxi across town. There were trolleys, but he hadn't acquainted himself with their schedules and, besides, taxis were faster. Now that time was a factor-he wanted to finish his business and return to Smithville-he could not afford to loiter. Jeff looked interestedly at the section of the city they were entering.

Downtown Ackerton was crowded, with land so precious that there was no room for any space at all between buildings. Even the more modest residential areas had houses close together and a bit of yard in front and back. This must be where the wealthy element lived. The houses were large and set back from the streets. By Ackerton standards, the lawns were very spacious, though all of them together wouldn't have offered a hill dweller as much room as he needed. They came to an area where there were no residences at all but only a few business places, and Jeff had a fleeting glimpse of one that interested him. The display windows were clear, but drapes hung behind them and Jeff thought he saw a tapestry displayed. He memorized the name; the Murchison Galleries.

The cabbie turned aside into a paved drive and halted his taxi beside a large building that had a distinct air of gentility. The taxi stopped and Jeff looked puzzled.

"I wanted the Jackson School." "This is it."

Jeff paid the driver, got out and looked around. Obviously a converted mansion, the Jackson School had none of the aloofness of the mansions they had passed.

Surrounded by green lawns and flower gardens, there was the same strong sense of being welcome that was so evident on Granny Wilson's hill. Jeff whistled. Johnny Blazer, who had lived in a cabin behind Smithville, hadn't stinted himself when he chose a school for his son. Jeff knew a little misgiving. It was his intention to see Dan back here when the school term opened. But could he afford it?

"Might as well find out," he murmured to himself.

Inside the main entrance, a pleasant girl looked up from a desk upon which was a typewriter, an inkwell with a tray of pens and a few papers. She smiled at Jeff.

"Yes?"

"I'd like to see-" Jeff tried and could not think of the titles given officials in private schools for boys. He grinned. "I'd like to discuss a youngster who probably would be in the sixth grade."

"Is he a student here?" "Yes."

"I'll call Mr. Nelson. Will you be seated, please?"

She talked into a speaking tube. Jeff seated himself on a comfortable divan, and as soon as he saw him, he approved of the man who came in. About fifty years old, he was short and inclined to stoutness. He wore a gray suit that fitted well and had been chosen with care. His face was flushed and his hair iron-gray. But the blue eyes that set his face off were gentle, understanding and wise. Jeff rose to meet him.

"Mr. Nelson?"

"Yes sir." His voice was soft and pleasant.

"My name's Jeff Tarrant," Jeff introduced himself. "I've come to talk to you about Dan Blazer."

Alert interest flooded the headmaster's face. "Oh, yes. Do you know where he is?"

"Yes. Let me tell you."

Mr. Nelson listened attentively while Jeff spoke of finding Dan in Johnny Blazer's cabin. Jeff told of Dan's fierce anger, and his unshakable determination to seek out whoever had killed his father and extract full vengeance. He spoke of his own part in it and of the paper-loaded shotgun shells. Jeff did not try to conceal the fact that he was a peddler, nor did he hide

Dan's interest in peddling. He told of his own hopes to find Johnny's murderer, let the law take its course, and of the effect he thought that would have on Dan.

For a moment after he finished, Mr. Nelson did not speak. Then he asked, "Where is the boy now?"

"I left him in very good hands. He will lack for nothing."

Mr. Nelson looked troubled. "What do you intend to do with him, Mr. Tarrant?"

"If I can afford it, I want to bring him back here when the fall term opens."

Mr. Nelson smiled gently. "Mr. Tarrant, when you looked up the Jackson School for Boys, I'm sure you saw nothing about our being restricted to wealthy boys only. We do have students, and I'll admit that they are of exceptional ability, who pay whatever their parents or guardians can afford."

"Where does Dan rate in that category?"

"Very highly. Very highly I assure you. An outstanding youngster, but your revelations were not a complete surprise."

"You expected him to run away?"

"I took him to his father's funeral," Mr. Nelson said softly. "He said little, but I knew what he was thinking. After he ran away, I wrote to the authorities in Smithville, but I've had no reply."

"That's my fault," Jeff admitted. "I told them that Dan was under my care and that I'd contact you personally."

"You did? By any chance did you have ideas about looking us over?" "I had that idea. And I had no intention of letting him come back if you

did not measure up."

"Oh! We do meet your standards?" Jeff smiled. "You're good enough."

"You might have brought Dan with you."

"I might also have put him in a cage," Jeff said wryly. "And if I kept him there for one, three, or ten years, he'd get out some time. When he did, he'd still go back and hunt whoever shot his father."

"How old are you, Mr. Tarrant?" "Going on nineteen."

"Would it be impertinent to ask your background?"

Jeff said quietly, "I lived in an orphanage until I was a little past fourteen. Then I ran away and worked at various jobs. Since quitting the last one, I've been a peddler."

"I see. And what do you hope to gain by sending this youngster back to us?"

Jeff still spoke quietly. "Sleep, easy sleep at night because I did not leave him alone when he had no one else to whom he could turn." "What does Dan think about it?"

"I haven't told him," Jeff grinned, "but I have a pact with him. Dan has agreed to do anything I say."

"Why?"

"He likes peddling, and he has an idea that he's going to throw in with me. I told him he couldn't unless he minded me."

"What are your plans for the future?"

"I haven't decided," Jeff said seriously. "But I like Smithville, and if things continue to get as well as they've started out, in the next three or four years I'll be able to build up a good business right in Smithville."

"I see. Do you have any ideas about Dan's 'throwing in' with you?" "Yes I do," Jeff confessed. "I like him and I'd like to have him; Tarrant

and Blazer would be a mighty good team. But first he must have an education." "Why?"

"So he'll know what I have never learned. I read as much as I can, but that's not as good as solid groundwork in school."

"If you pay for his education, would you insist on his later services?" "No, he can choose his own way."

"You're willing to be responsible for him on such a basis?" "Yes, sir. Wh-what is your tuition fee?"

"Mr. Blazer paid-" Mr. Nelson named half the sum Jeff had expected. "What do you wish to have me do?"

"I want only your written confirmation that Dan is in my care."

"May I also say that you are to return him to us by September fourteenth?"

"Certainly."

"All right. Miss Jackson, may I borrow your desk?"

The confirming letter in an inside pocket, Jeff strode happily out of the school. It had all been much simpler than he had thought possible, but Mr. Nelson was an understanding person. Jeff knew that he himself had undergone one of the most severe examinations of his life-and had passed it. Relieved about Dan, he could now give his whole attention to the business at hand.

It was a long way to the Kennard, but Jeff did not want to hail or phone for a taxi as yet because the neighborhood, and the stores he had seen, interested him. He walked back the way he had come, saw the stores ahead, and halted in front of the Murchison Galleries.

He wanted to assure himself that he had seen what he thought he had seen, and it was there. In the window, somehow accentuated by the very simplicity of its surroundings, was a tapestry that depicted a bowl of crocuses in bloom. Though he did not know a great deal about tapestries, Jeff realized that this was a very fine one. But mentally he compared it to Granny's, and decided that hers was better. Jeff entered the galleries.

Though only fair-sized, the arrangement of the interior loaned an illusion of spaciousness and its air was one of quiet refinement. There were paintings on the walls and others on easels, and without examining them too closely, Jeff knew that the way they were placed added much to their effectiveness. He turned to meet the man coming toward him and was greeted with a pleasant, "Good morning."

He said it as though he were welcoming a guest into his house, and Jeff responded in kind. "Good morning. I think you may save my life!"

"Indeed?" The man arched his brows. "You hardly seem on the verge of expiring."

"I really am, though. You do know something about tapestries?" "A bit." The man smiled indulgently. "What do you wish?"

Jeff unrolled Granny's The Last Supper and held it up for inspection. "I must find the exact duplicate of this." "May I see it?"

The man took the tapestry, felt its texture, turned it over and examined it at arm's length. His eyes hardened ever so slightly. Lowering the tapestry, he wrinkled his brow in thought.

"Perhaps we may help you, Mr.-" "Tarrant," Jeff supplied. "Jeffrey Tarrant."

"I'm Raold Murchison. You wish us to find a duplicate of this?"

"If you can," Jeff wanted twenty-five dollars but decided he might as well try for more. "It's worth a hundred dollars."

"How soon must you have it, Mr. Tarrant?"

"Tomorrow noon's the deadline," Jeff said ruefully. "Just think! I've been in

Ackerton almost a week before I found you."

"Where are you staying?" "The Kennard. Room sixteen."

"May we retain this until tomorrow at noon?" "Of course, naturally you will-"

"Naturally. I would not ask you to leave it without a receipt. Will you be at the Kennard at noon?"

"I'll make it a point to be there."

"I shall phone you then, Mr. Tarrant, and advise you concerning our success or failure."

He gave Jeff a receipt and noted his name and room number. Jeff left the galleries, knowing that he had taken a gamble. But who hoped to win had to take chances. With nothing else to do, he gave the rest of the day and most of the next morning to wandering about Ackerton. He returned to his room at twenty to twelve, and exactly twenty minutes later his phone rang.

"Mr. Tarrant," it was the desk clerk, "there's a Mr. Murchison here to see you."

"Send him in."

Jeff opened the door for Raold Murchison, and no matter where he stood, he would still be master of the Murchison Galleries.

"I came in person, Mr. Tarrant, because that seemed best." "Indeed?"

"Yes, we succeeded in locating the exact duplicate of your tapestry."

Jeff gave thanks for his ability to wear a poker face when such was in order. If the Murchison Galleries had located the twin of Granny's The Last Supper, Granny had made it. And Raold Murchison wouldn't even know how to talk to her.

Murchison smiled tentatively. "In the process of finding the duplicate, we also found a customer who is enamoured of the pair."

"Those things happen."

"I assume that you have a customer who will pay you at least two hundred dollars?"

Jeff made no comment. It was Murchison's privilege to assume anything he wished. The art dealer continued, "I am prepared to offer you a hundred and twenty-five dollars for yours."

Jeff's heart leaped but his face revealed nothing. Obviously, somewhere among his wealthy neighbors, Raold Murchison, just as Jeff had hoped, had known the exact person who would appreciate such a tapestry. Naturally, he would sell it for more than the price offered Jeff, but he was entitled to a profit, too. Hiding his elation, Jeff frowned.

"It isn't the price I thought I'd get."

"But you cannot sell yours without a duplicate?"

Jeff looked away without answering. Murchison waited expectantly.

Finally Jeff looked back. "Well, all right," he agreed. "How about taking another tapestry?" Jeff asked. "Oh, you have another?"

Jeff showed him The Fall of Satan. Raold Murchison examined it and turned to Jeff.

"A fair enough piece and I'll speculate. Shall we say fifty dollars?" "Let's say seventy-five?"

"I'm taking a chance but-Will you accept my personal check?" "Certainly."

Raold Murchison wrote a check and waved it in the air until it dried. "If you should be in Ackerton again, Mr. Tarrant, the Murchison Galleries are ever ready to be of service."

He left and Jeff leaped high to click his heels in the air. He had hoped to get fifty dollars for both tapestries. He had two hundred and a strong hint that more tapestries would be welcome. He fairly danced down to the desk.

"When is the next train for Delview?" he asked.

The clerk consulted a time table. "Five-three." "Thanks."

Jeff ran out on the street and hailed a taxi.

"The nearest place where I can buy a kitten," he directed, "and stay with me. I want you all afternoon."

"Sure, Bub."

Half past four, and five pet shops later, Jeff found what he wanted. Of three white Angora kittens in the window, one was almost the twin of Granny's departed pet. It watched Jeff shyly, and arched its back against his hand. Then it promptly proceeded to bite his finger. Plainly it was a kitten with character.

"I want it!" Jeff told the astonished proprietor. "Put it in a cage or something because it's going on the train!"

Lifted into a second-hand bird cage, the kitten spat its indignation and fell to swiping at shadows with a silky paw. Jeff laid five dollars, the requested price, on the counter and thrust his hand into the pocket where the miniatures lay.

"Present for you," he said, scattering them across the counter. He rushed to the cab. "Hotel Kennard and don't spare the gasoline. I have to be at the station by five-two!"

He made it with a whole minute to spare.

10. BOMBSHELL

Dan Blazer, going up the trail toward Granny Wilson's with the shotgun in one hand and Pal's leash in the other, was a little angry and more than a little resentful. Though Jeff had said that Dan was going to take care of Granny, the boy had convinced himself that he was actually to be taken care of. He resented it because he and Jeff had a pact-Dan had promised to do anything Jeff said-but Jeff seemed to have forgotten. If he wanted to stay at Granny's, he had only to say so and nothing else was necessary. Dan turned to pull the balky Pal along.

"Come on!" he ordered. "Come on, Pal! Jeff's going to Ackerton and he doesn't want either you or me with him!"

Pal, who had wanted to go with Jeff but who was beginning to get the idea that he was not supposed to, stopped straining back on the leash. He was not wholly abandoned, as he had been when Johnny went away, and that was a comfort.

Dan brightened a little. Jeff had not only let him have the shotgun and the six shells but had insisted that he take them. The very fact that Jeff had trusted him with both made him feel more like a man and less like a little boy. He gripped the shotgun tightly. Some day he would look down the rib that separated its two barrels and see the man who had shot his father. Dan's eyes flashed, then softened. That day must not be now; he had promised Jeff that he wouldn't shoot anybody and Jeff was very smart. Dan skipped along.

Save for the one dark cloud, the future glowed with bright promise. Jeff had promised to make a peddler of him and that would be the ideal life. Dan thought of it during his waking moments and dreamed of it in his sleep. All he had to do in order to make his dreams come true was obey Jeff, and that was a small price to pay for the reward it offered. Jeff was all-wise, all-good, all- powerful, and maybe he had really sent Dan to take care of Granny.

When Granny's green hill came in sight, Dan's spirits were almost completely lifted. The fact that he wished so desperately to take a man's part helped convince him that he was taking one, and he forgot his resentment to greet Granny with a smile.

"Good morning, Granny." "Dan! My land! Where's Jeff?"

"Gone to Ackerton and he'll be gone for some time. He-" Dan hesitated. "He sent me and Pal up to look after you while he's away."

Granny reacted precisely as Jeff had thought she would. "Now that was a kindly thought! I really miss a man around the house. Come in and let me set you a dish of cookies."

Granny's wholehearted acceptance of himself and his mission removed most of the lingering suspicion Dan retained that Granny was really supposed to take care of him. He swelled with newfound importance and felt a profound gratitude toward Jeff for sending him on a man's job. The cookies Granny set before him were tangible proof that taking care of her would not be without its rewards. With the appetite of a dragon and the digestion of a goat, and despite his substantial breakfast, Dan finished all the cookies and wished there were more. But it would hardly be polite to ask.

"I can stay until Jeff gets back, Granny," he said. "You won't have to worry while I'm here."

"I won't," she asserted. "I just won't fret even one particle. It's such a comfort to have you. What's Jeff doing in Ackerton?"

"Trading. We've been working pretty hard and now he has to trade everything we got." Dan thought wistfully of Jeff, who in the boy's mind was nine feet tall and possessed all the capacities of a wizard. "He'll do all right, too. Those city people, they're not near as smart as Jeff."

"They couldn't be," Granny agreed solemnly. "That Jeff, he's man all through."

"We're partners," Dan said. "Partners in everything. Any of those Whitneys been bothering you, Granny?"

"Not of late." Granny looked a bit puzzled. "Why do you ask about the Whitneys?"

"Because," Dan said fiercely, "one of them shot my pop and soon's Jeff and me find out which one, we're going to shoot him!"

"My land! How you talk!"

Dan felt suddenly that he was a little boy again, and justly censured by an adult for lack of wisdom. He all but blushed. "We're not going to do it right away."

"That's nice," Granny said.

"Now I have to take care of you. What needs taking care of first?" "You might go see that no pesky thing's troublin' my sheep."

Pal at his heels, Dan raced down to where the fat sheep were at their endless task of cropping grass. They looked at him with mildly surprised eyes and continued to crop. Dan circled the sheep three times, petted the gentle creatures, and was more than a little disappointed because there seemed to be no immediate need of his protective services. But he did not lose hope, there was still a lot of Granny's hill left.

Molly, Granny's placid old cow, and Ephraim, Granny's mule, were well off as the sheep. Dan sighed, then became a little excited when four blackbirds winged out of the trees to scratch in Granny's garden. He stalked them carefully. But before he could come near enough, Pal charged the blackbirds and sent them in jittery flight back to the trees.

Dan circled the foot of the hill, looking hard for something from which Granny should be protected. But all he found was a cottontail rabbit that confounded the fleet Pal by ducking into a burrow three inches in front of his nose. Dan wandered back to Granny's house just in time for lunch.

That, consisting of bread much softer and better than any Abel Tarkman sold, butter, delicately-spiced strawberry preserves, goblets of milk, and a crisp apple turnover smothered in cream, was better than any Dan had eaten, even at the Jackson School for Boys.

Suddenly homesick, he thought of the school and all it had meant to him, then put the thought behind him. He had left the school because he was driven by a mission that would not let him rest and would never permit him to have peace until it was fulfilled. Until it was, he must think of nothing else; he shouldn't even think seriously of going peddling with Jeff but he couldn't help that. Then his faith restored itself. Jeff was all-wise and all-powerful. Jeff had promised him that justice would be done. Dan was a bit ashamed of his doubts Unable to swallow another bite, he pushed his plate back and lingered

over it. Granny, who hadn't had a hungry boy to satisfy in far too long, was shaping an apple pie at the table and Dan's eyes lingered on her. The big wood stove cast a pleasant glow into the room, and tantalizing odors promised much to come. Dan licked his lips, the faint beginning of fresh hunger rising on the very heels of the meal he had just eaten.

Dan wrinkled his brows. He had been sent to look after Granny, and look after her he would. But she didn't seem to need any looking-after right now and the forest surrounding the hill was an inviting place. He asked, "Is everything all right, Granny?"

"Land! It's right as rain since you got here. Haven't felt this safe in a dog's age."

"Would you still feel safe if Pal and me went down in the woods this afternoon?"

"Can you beat that? I was just about to ask you if you would! What you goin' to do there, Dan?"

"Look around and make sure nothing's lurking too near."

"Good! Good! If you can spare the time, you might bring a few trout for us to sup on."

"Oh, boy!"

Dan whooped from his chair. With Pal bustling at his heels, he ran out to the garden. He loved to fish, his father had taught him how to catch trout, and Granny's accustomed tackle, a hook and line tied to a willow pole, hung over the door. In the spring's damp overflow Dan grubbed until he had filled his

pocket with fat worms. Then he snatched the pole from over the doorway and raced down to the little stream that from the hilltop wound like a silver ribbon through the forest.

He strung a worm on his hook, crawled cautiously up to a pool and dropped the worm gently, watching with bated breath the ripples that spread. A trout surged from the depths, struck viciously, and Dan drew his wriggling catch in. Deftly he slipped it onto a willow stringer.

Stringer in one hand, pole in the other, he sneaked up to another pool and caught another trout. Mindful of the pies Granny was making, he decided that he needed no more than two trout for himself because his appetite must be saved for more important things. Granny might eat three. Dan had four trout on his stringer when Pal growled.

Hackles raised, ears alert, nose questing, he peered upstream. Dan stopped, not knowing what was coming but sure that Pal wouldn't growl for no reason. Dragging the dog with him, the boy slipped into the brush and a moment later Barr Whitney appeared.

He was fishing, too, but instead of a willow stringer he carried a buckskin creel into which he slipped trout as he caught them. Dan held his breath and at the same time did his best to control his rising rage. He wished mightily that he had brought the shotgun, but so far there had been no indication that he would need it. Watching Barr come nearer, he made himself very small.

If he did not move, maybe Barr wouldn't see him. But when the man came opposite Dan, he swerved and splashed across the creek. Trousers dripping, seeming like some wet monster that emerged from the water, he had only a glance for the growling Pal. But he thrust a hand inside his shirt and the boy knew that he had a weapon of some sort concealed there. Dan quieted the growling Pal by gently stroking him.

"What be ye doin' here, boy?"

Dan glared. "I don't talk to no blamed Whitneys!" Barr's eyes clouded. "Mind your tongue, boy."

"I won't mind it! But one of you Whitneys will wish you'd minded yourselves when Jeff and me find out who killed my pop!"

"We will?"

"Yes, you will! And me and Jeff are on the track." "You be?"

Jeff's image came to stand beside Dan, so that he no longer felt small, alone and so terribly frightened. With his friend beside him, he could do anything. "Ha!" he exploded. "You think Jeff's a peddler, but he's not." Dan cast desperately for an apt description and thought of the most awesome image his mind could conjure up. "He's a policeman. A real policeman. Now he's gone

into Ackerton for more policemen, and soon's he gets some, they'll get every one of you darned Whitneys. You wait! You'll be sorry, Jeff said so!"

"So-o," Barr Whitney purred. "So-o."

"Aren't you-Aren't you going to do anything to me?"

"Can't think of ary I'd do, 'cept mebbe string you on the hook an' use you for bait."

No longer interested in fishing, Barr Whitney splashed back across the creek and disappeared in the forest. Immensely gratified, Dan watched him go.

He'd told those Whitneys.

Except that the fluffy kitten did not like the bird cage and expressed his dislike with frequent far-carrying "miaouws" that attracted the attention of everyone else in the day coach, Jeff's trip from Ackerton to Delview was almost routine. It was not entirely so because twice the conductor threatened either to take the kitten into the baggage car or throw Jeff and his luggage off the train. Both times a chorus of dissent rose from the six other passengers in the car. The train did not make as many stops as the one from Delview to Ackerton had, but it was equally slow and the kitten provided diversion.

When they finally reached Delview, the kitten stood erect and glared at everything in sight. Obviously he was a creature of great character and he would fit in perfectly on Granny's hill.

Pack on his back and the caged kitten dangling from his right hand, Jeff strode down Delview's main street. He had decided, as he usually did, to guide himself by whatever circumstances seemed to require. If he felt too tired, he would put up at one of Delview's two hotels overnight. But the events of the day, particularly his astounding success with Granny's tapestries, had roused him to a pitch of enthusiasm so high that he was not at all tired. The star-lighted night was ideal for walking and Jeff made up his mind to go right through to Smithville. He should get there some time in the early morning hours. He was anxious to see Dan again and to watch Granny's eyes when he told her what he had done with her tapestries.

He was hungry, but the first cafe he entered was one of Delview's exclusive eating places and the late diners who still lingered there stared in horror at the caged kitten. A waiter asked him to leave, and Jeff did not feel like arguing the point. The second cafe, not so pretentious and presided over by a fat man with a completely bald head and a clean apron, was less particular. Jeff laid his pack down, put the cage on a chair and ordered,

"Steak, fried potatoes and coffee. Heavy on all three and a saucer of milk for the kitten."

"Sure, bud, sure."

The fat man poked a pudgy finger at the kitten, who crouched in the cage and evidently imagined himself unseen. He sprang suddenly, and when he leaped against the cage's door, it burst open. The kitten slithered through,

jumped to the table, gave everything in the restaurant a haughty look, scrambled to Jeff's shoulder and began to purr contentedly.

"Cute lil' feller!" the fat man said admiringly. "Why do you keep him caged?"

Jeff saw opportunity. The cage had been only a means for getting the

kitten from Ackerton to Granny's. But if the kitten preferred Jeff's shoulder, he was welcome to ride there. The fat man was obviously interested in the cage.

"Usually I don't," Jeff admitted. "I got the cage to bring him through from Ackerton." He added, as though it were an afterthought, "Darn' thing cost me two dollars."

"Hmm. Need the cage any more?" "I don't know."

"My wife's been lookin' for such. She keeps birds. What'll you take for it?"

Jeff forsook bargaining. His pack was full, and since the kitten seemed

happy on his shoulder, he did not want to carry the cage to Smithville. "Swap for the dinner."

"It's a swap."

The fat man, who apparently was also the cook, went into the kitchen. He came back with a platter containing a huge steak and an ample supply of potatoes. He also had a mug of coffee that held at least a pint. The kitten scrambled from Jeff's shoulder to the table top, turned up his nose at the saucer of milk placed before him, and looked appealingly at Jeff's steak.

Jeff grinned. This kitten knew what he wanted and was willing to try for it. Jeff fed him a small piece of steak, then another, and a third. Only when Jeff firmly refused to give him any more did he turn and lap up every bit of the milk. When it was time to go, he climbed back on Jeff's shoulder and pressed his naked nose and pads against his friend's neck, where they would stay warm.

Jeff walked swiftly through the cool night, stopping every hour or so to rest. He enjoyed every second of it.

Dawn was faint in the sky when they came to Smithville, and rising and stretching on Jeff's shoulder, the kitten greeted it with a hearty miaouw.

"Who's there?" It was the constable, Bill Ellis. "Jeff Tarrant," Jeff called.

"I've been waiting for you."

Even though the constable was only half-seen, there was about him a great hesitation that was mingled with a certain furtiveness as he came through the darkness. Jeff waited, more than a little surprised.

Bill Ellis came nearer and whispered, "Where you been?" "Why-Ackerton."

The kitten miaouwed again and Bill Ellis took a backward step. "What's that?"

"Just a kitten that I'm bringing to Granny Wilson."

There was vast urgency in Bill Ellis' voice as he said, "Don't go there. Turn around and get out of the hills. Don't come back." "Why?"

"Never mind why. Just go." "I'm going to Granny's."

Bill Ellis' shrug was more sensed than seen. "You got a gun?" "Why-no."

"Where is it?"

"At Granny's. By the way, here's the letter from the school."

He took the letter from an inside pocket and handed it over. Bill Ellis accepted it, but it seemed unimportant.

"If you won't run," he said, "get to Granny's and get your gun while darkness lasts. Don't go anywhere again without it."

"But-"

"Do as I say and-" there was a definite note of fear in Bill Ellis' voice-"don't tell anybody I told you."

He turned and walked swiftly away, as though the peddler had suddenly become an outcast or tainted being with whom he must not have further contact. Jeff stood a moment, completely bewildered. Why this unexpected warning? What had come into the hills since he'd left for Ackerton? Why was Bill Ellis afraid?

Jeff called softly, "Bill."

The constable waited. Jeff trotted to him. "Tell me some more."

"I've told you enough. Don't go out unless you can protect yourself. I can do nothing for you, and the best thing you can do is run."

"Nobody would gun down an unarmed man." "Don't be a fool."

"I see. Bill, did Johnny Blazer have a gun when he was found?" "No. Leave me now. It's growing lighter."

Jeff resumed his journey up the road, and the kitten stretched all four paws against his neck. Shaking his head uncertainly, he did not turn aside when he came to Johnny Blazer's cabin. Bill Ellis had told him to get to Granny's and arm himself-before daylight. He'd better do it.

The sun was just rising when Jeff came to Granny's green hill, and he heard Pal's happy roar of welcome. He quickened his steps, and even on this hill of peace he had an uncomfortable feeling that he was watched by furtive eyes. Johnny Blazer had been shot down in cold blood.

At the door, he composed himself. Granny and Dan must not be worried. When he entered the cabin, an ecstatic Pal flung himself forward and

Jeff tickled the big dog's ears. He turned to meet Granny, who always rose with the sun.

"Hiya, Granny!" He plucked the kitten from his shoulder. "I brought you a present!"

"Oh, the love!"

Granny cuddled the kitten against her cheek. Knowing experienced hands and instantly liking Granny almost as much as she loved him, the kitten licked her cheek with a pink tongue and fell to purring. Rubbing sleepy eyes, pajama-clad Dan came from his bedroom.

"Jeff!"

"Hi, Dan!"

"My land!" Granny's eyes sparkled like sunshine on dewdrops. "I'll make some breakfast right away."

"What'd you see in Ackerton?" Dan asked eagerly. "What'd you see in Ackerton, Jeff."

"Hang on to your horses!" Jeff laughed. "I'll tell you in good time.

Granny, I sold your tapestries." "Did you now?"

"Couldn't get what they're worth, though," Jeff said sadly. "Land! Had no idea they were worth anything."

"I got two hundred dollars."

"Jeff!" Granny almost dropped the kitten.

"I did, Granny. Four times as much as I told you I'd get." "But-"

"And there's a place for more."

Granny stroked the kitten and there was a look of near sadness in her eyes. After a moment she said gently, "It seems almost sinful, that much for aught so small."

"It's not," Jeff assured her. "The man who bought them from me will make a profit, too."

"He can do that and welcome he is. Land! Who would have thought it?

Two hundred dollars! Half would do me for a year." "All would do you for two years."

Granny shook her head. "No, Jeff. For sixty-four years I've abided here and never had a hundred dollars all at once. Never missed it, either, 'cept when Enos was sick. I might have paid a doctor for him. If you see fit to give me half, I'll take it should I have need of aught that is not at my hand. Half is yours."

Jeff hesitated. He worked for profit, but somehow it hadn't seemed right to make any on Granny. Still, as far as she was concerned, a hundred dollars was a vast sum and obviously she had gone as far as she intended to go.

Granny laughed. "We'll leave it that way and I'll have more ta-Oh, hang! I keep forgettin' the name. More cloths the next time you go. It seems a mort of pay for what pleasures me so dear. Now I'll rouse up some eatables."

She baked delicious pancakes, fried a heaping platter of sausage and put them on the table. Granny and Dan listened intently, prompting him if he omitted the smallest detail, as Jeff told everything about his trip to Ackerton.

When he had finished, he looked pointedly at Dan, declaring, "And finally, I arranged for you to go back to school in September."

"I'm not going," Dan said firmly.

"You must go," Jeff urged. "Dan, you and I can build up a good business here, but unless we always want to carry peddlers' packs, one of us has to know business methods. The place to learn them is in school."

"I want to carry a pack."

"You'll have your chance; it isn't going to work that fast. Think of ten or maybe even fifteen years from now. Imagine a trading post in Smithville and a store in Ackerton with BLAZER AND TARRANT ENTERPRISES in gold letters a foot high across both of 'em." Jeff grinned. "We could cut out the Ltd. If we were partners, we wouldn't be limited any more."

Dan said stubbornly, "I can't go."

"Could you if-if you were satisfied about your pop?" Dan hesitated. "You promise, Jeff?"

"I promise." "Before I go?" "Before you go."

"Then," Dan sighed, "I reckon I can go back."

"Good," Jeff said quickly. "Now I want you to stay here and keep Pal with you. I'm going away for a little while."

"Where you going, Jeff?"

"Into Smithville and I'm taking the shotgun." "I'm going with you."

"Not this time. I have to go alone." "But-"

"It's wisdom he speaks," Granny said softly. "You bide here, Dan." "Well-When you coming back, Jeff?"

"I don't know exactly. But I will be back." "You take a care."

"Now don't be fretting about me." Jeff grinned.

But he was not grinning when, with the shotgun in his right hand and the paper-loaded shells in his pocket, he left Granny's house and hit the trail back to Smithville. The time for a showdown was here.

Jeff planned as he walked. He had always known that he would stop wandering and settle down when and if he found a place he liked well enough, and he liked these hills. Though he'd never been able to imagine himself confined to any one small spot, the hills were not small. They presented a challenge he liked. The fact that he'd have to fight for his right to be here, and that there were problems to be solved, was not extraordinary. He'd always had to fight and there'd always been problems.

Jeff knew suddenly what he had never known before, his whole life had been almost desperately lonely. He hadn't thought of it in such a light because there had been no fair basis for comparison. Never having been anything except lonely, he could not know what it was to be otherwise. Now he had Dan, Granny, Pal, and a genuine love for all three. They were his, and having them was good.

He had no illusions about becoming very rich, for he saw no great wealth in the offing. There would be a comfortable living, with always enough variety so that there would be continual zest. The hill people needed what the outside world could offer, but without someone to act as intermediary, they had almost no chance of getting it. Those of the outside world delighted in the products of the hills, and they had the money to pay for them. Nobody would be cheated.

Jeff put these thoughts behind him. First things must always be first, and before he did anything else he had to meet, and fight, whoever was gunning for him. For Dan's sake, and his own conscience, he must bring to justice whoever had shot Johnny Blazer. He could do neither with words, for it had come to guns. But before he could use the shotgun effectively, he had to have live ammunition for it. He wished mightily that he had left at least one shell loaded.

Wanting only to see if anything had been disturbed there, Jeff swung aside when he came to Johnny Blazer's cabin. He entered.

Inside, each man armed with a rifle that swung at once to cover Jeff, were Pete, Barr, Yancey, Grant and Dabb Whitney.

11. THE TALKING TREE

They stood along the wall, unkempt and untidy, but there was something about them that was as cold and deadly as the whine of a bullet or the fangs of a viper. They were lean as weasels, and as fast. The rifles they held, from the repeating carbines belonging to Barr, Yancey, Dabb and Grant, to Pete's single-shot fifty caliber, seemed a part of them and they had grown up with those rifles. These were men who had no shots to waste and who therefore must make every one count. They would be shamed if they shot a turkey or grouse anywhere except through the head and they had only raucous jeers for whoever was unable to shoot as well.

"Turn 'raound!" Pete ordered gruffly.

"Not here ya fool!" Barr countermanded the order. "A fair half of Smithville'll come a'racin'."

Pete sneered. "Let 'em come. They won't find us."

"No!" Obviously Barr was in command. "This goes my way."

Jeff stood, cold and shaken and knowing that, when he walked into the cabin, he had walked into his own death. These must be the men about whom Bill Ellis had warned him. But why should the Whitneys want to kill him? Summoning all his past experience with Tarrant Enterprises, Ltd., which had taught him to try to appear outwardly cool in the hottest of spots, Jeff did his best to seem not only calm but to take full command of the situation.

"You're in my cabin," he said quietly.

"We knaow," Pete's eyes were venom-laden, "but you won't be needin' it fer long."

The rest of the Whitneys said nothing. Jeff studied them and tried, by reading their faces, to determine his next act.

81

Pete, so poisoned with hatred that it distorted his face, offered nothing. Yancey, Dabb and Grant might be swayed if it were not for Barr. Dominating the rest, and with them, at the same time he stood apart from them. He was strong, Pete was weak-and for that very reason extremely dangerous. The rest needed leadership. But while there was no lust in Barr's eyes, neither was there any mercy. Jeff looked steadily at him and kept his voice quiet.

"What's it about?"

"We liked ya, peddler." Barr's voice was very grave. "We liked ya an' you traded fair with your goods. But there's no bit of room in these hills for a policeman."

"Policeman!" Jeff exploded.

"We know," Barr seemed downcast, as though someone he trusted had betrayed him. "The boy told us."

"Told you what?"

"All-an' 'twill serve ya naught to plead or ask pardon. If you're a man, be one now."

Jeff's head whirled. Apparently, while he was in Ackerton, one or more of the Whitneys had met Dan and the boy had spun some fantastic tale. Jeff looked over his captors again and saw only unyielding determination. He took a deep breath before he spoke.

"What did Dan tell you?"

"Enough," Barr grunted. "We had the truth from a babe's mouth." "But-"

Dabb interrupted. "What made ye set your mind on the thought that a Whitney kil't Blazer?"

"Didn't you?"

"We do not pry into killin's," Barr said. "You erred when you did."

Another piece fitted into the puzzle. Evidently Dan had told whoever it was he had met that he and Jeff were out to avenge Johnny, and doubtless he'd said that Jeff was an officer. Jeff pondered Dabb's question and Barr's comment. It was possible, even probable, that only his killer knew who had shot Johnny. Whoever was guilty would be a fool if he was anything except close-mouthed about it.

"Leave us shoot him," Pete said nasally. "'Twill serve naught to do elsewise."

"I said we'd wait," Barr growled.

Jeff breathed a little easier. The Whitneys intended to shoot him, but not immediately and he wondered what they were waiting for and why. Perhaps, as Barr had mentioned, they were too close to Smithville, and in order to remain unseen, perhaps they would wait until night to take him out. Maybe there were other reasons, but evidently he had a little time. Jeff took a shot in the dark.

"I'll be missed in Ackerton."

"We know," Barr muttered. "The boy said it all."

Jeff moistened dry lips with his tongue. His chance shot had ricocheted; whatever story Dan had concocted tied in with Jeff's trip to Ackerton. He had to think his way out of this.

"People will be looking for me."

"They won't find you," Barr promised. "But could be they'll find us." Jeff said pointedly, "Five against one?"

"You had a shotgun when you come in."

"And if I'd known who was waiting, I'd have come shooting. But you can all cheer up. Maybe those who look for me won't expect to need guns, and

you can take them just like you did me. Maybe they won't even have guns. Then you can shoot them down from ambush, like you did Johnny Blazer!"

Six pairs of eyes regarded him, and only Pete's remained unchanged. The rest shifted from deliberate purposefulness to cold fury, and Barr's face turned white. His lips tautened, and he bit his words off and spat them at Jeff.

"Ye lie!"

"I do not lie!"

Swiftly Barr closed the distance between them. His left hand snaked forward and his open palm struck Jeff's cheek. It was not a blow that a man might offer a worthy antagonist, but an insulting slap. Barr's eyes were glowing coals.

"Ye lie, policeman! Nary a man in the hills shot Blazer thataway!" Jeff snarled back, "I don't lie and I can prove it!"

His face still white, Barr stepped back. He jerked his rifle to shooting position and lowered it reluctantly. Tense as stretched buckskin, he studied Jeff and snapped, "Say those words ag'in!"

"Johnny Blazer not only had no gun when he was shot, but whoever shot him was hiding when he did it!" Jeff pronounced each word very slowly and very clearly, as though he were rehearsing a careful speech.

"How d'ye know he lacked aught to shoot back?"

"I-" Jeff thought of Bill Ellis and caught himself in time. "I saw someone who found him on my Ackerton trip. Johnny had no gun when they picked him up."

"Shut up!" Barr whirled furiously on his cousin who had started to speak. He said, more to himself than to anyone else, "Blazer's guns was found in his cabin."

Jeff laughed tauntingly. "You hillbillies are brave men! Now all you have to do is admit that whoever shot Johnny was hiding in the brush."

Still furious, Barr regarded him steadily. "How do ya know that?" "All I had to do was look."

"What'd ya look at?"

Jeff answered contemptuously, "I wouldn't expect any of you to think that far, but the bullet went clear through Johnny. There are enough trees and shrubs around so that it had to nick one of them. It's easy to figure the angle it came from."

Jeff held his breath. He himself had not thought of this until now, but it had to be right. Johnny Blazer was a woodsman. If whoever shot him had been in the open, Johnny would have seen him. Because he was unarmed, he probably would have died anyhow. But he would have died in the brush for he would at least have tried to escape.

Slow-thinking Dabb digested Jeff's statement and spoke solemnly. "Hit's right, Barr. None among us thought to look."

Barr was momentarily bewildered. "None saw the need." "But need there might be."

"Go look, Dabb."

"I'll gao, too," Pete offered. "Dabb's goin'."

Rifle in the crook of his arm, Dabb left the cabin. Jeff waited uneasily. Dabb's education might be a bit short in the conjugation of verbs and the more complex forms of mathematics, but it had taught him all about ballistics. When he came back he would know whether or not Johnny had been shot from ambush.

If he hadn't been-Jeff looked at Barr's stormy eyes and shuddered.

Twenty minutes later, Dabb returned. He came slowly, and somewhat shrunkenly, as though he had been both derided and belittled. He stood in the doorway, not looking at the rest, and when he spoke his voice was muffled and reluctant.

"Hit's true, Barr. Hit's true enough. Whosoever shot Blazer was crouchin' in a little patch of evergreens a hunnert an' fifty steps from the road." He said, as though that was vastly important, "With my own eyes I saw his crouch. He broke some twigs the better to see."

Something came into the cabin with him, an unseen but heavy and mournful something that seemed, within itself, to rob everyone of the power of speech. The Whitneys looked sidewise at each other and Barr spoke slowly,

"Thus ye saw?" "Thus I saw."

"Whar did the lead strike?"

"The tree," Dabb answered dully. "Hit's buried in the tree."

There was silence which Barr broke with a soul-desolated cry, "This day I know shame!"

They were weighted as though by heavy burdens, and Jeff understood why they scourged themselves. By the cowardly action of one of their number, something they could never get back had been taken from all of them. They must hang their heads because among them walked a man who was not a man. Jeff rubbed salt into their wounds.

"You can all be proud of yourselves."

It was as though they did not hear. This terrible crime, this heinous sin, had been committed, but they did not want to believe.

Grant said hopefully, "Maybe 'twar an outlander." "'Twar no outlander," Barr muttered. "'Twas a hill man."

Jeff trembled, fired with another idea. If the tree could talk, he had thought, it might tell who shot Johnny Blazer. The tree could talk!

"Are you afraid to find out who did it?" he challenged. Barr glowered at him. "An' how do we do that!"

"Dig the bullet out of the tree."

"Pay nao heed to him!" Pete intoned. "He would but tangle us an' lead us from him."

"Hold your tongue!" Barr ordered gruffly. "No man walks safe with one among us who shoots men as he would a varmint! Get the bullet, Dabb!"

Dabb left a second time and Jeff hoped his wildly beating heart could not be heard. To these mountain men killing was right, as long as men met in a fair fight.

But it was soul-blackening, the extreme depths of degradation, to kill as Johnny Blazer's killer had, and that killer was about to be known. Only one rifle could have fired the fatal shot, and the hill men would recognize that bullet and know who had fired it. Or would they? Four of the Whitneys present carried thirty caliber rifles and there must be more in the hills. Jeff's hopes alternately rose and waned.

Then Dabb came back and held up the leaden slug so all could see. Four pairs of eyes swung accusingly on Pete. Mushrooming where it had struck Johnny and then the tree, the slug still retained its shape where it had fitted its brass shell. There could be no mistake; it was fifty caliber.

Sweat broke out on Pete's forehead. "Hit-Hit-'Twarn't me!" Barr spat, "'Twar you!"

"He-he stole pelts out'en my traps!" "You met him unfair!"

Pete half screamed. "He had a rifle an' shot afore I did!" Barr said relentlessly, "Whar was his rifle?"

"I-I brought it back here!"

"He had no rifle! You lay like a whiskered cat afore a mouse's den an' gave him no fairness. Do not add a lie to cowardice."

Jeff said eagerly, "Now you know, Barr. Now all of you know, and Dan did tell part of the truth. I promised him that we'd find out who shot his father. It was all we wanted and all we will want. I am not a policeman."

Barr looked squarely at him. "So you say."

"It's true. Go to Ackerton and find out what I did there. And think a little. Neither the Whitneys nor anyone else can take the law into their own hands and forever keep it there. Do the right thing now."

"An' what is that?"

"Take Pete into Smithville and turn him over to Bill Ellis. He'll get a fair trial."

"Pah!" Yancey exploded. "Give our kin into the law's keep? 'Tis best to shoot him ourselves!"

"Stop the talkin'." Barr was still looking at Jeff. "You say ye are a peddler an' naught else?"

"I say so."

"Yet, you saw fit to beholden yourself to the boy? You took it upon yourself to tell him you'd settle with whosoever shot his father?"

"I did."

"Then, be ye peddler or policeman, you shall." "What do you mean?"

"We'll bide here through the day," Barr pronounced. "With the night we shall go to a cabin on Trilley Ridge. You have a shotgun an'," Barr inclined a contemptuous head toward Pete, "he has a rifle. With the dawn, both at the same time, ye'll walk on Trilley Ridge. If you come down the ridge, peddler, ye'll be free to come an' go amongst us. If Pete comes down it, he has a twenty- four hours to leave the hills. I shall sit with ye in the cabin. Grant, Dabb an' Yancey shall be at the foot of Trilley Ridge, to shoot should one of ye flee rather than fight."

Grant, Dabb and Yancey nodded solemn agreement. Jeff's head reeled. With tomorrow's dawn, he was to fight a death duel with Pete Whitney. Barr would be with them all night to make sure that things went according to his fantastic plan. Dabb, Grant and Yancey would be waiting to kill whoever violated the terms of the duel. If Jeff won, even though he would be privileged to remain in the hills, he would have killed a man. Regardless of what happened or who won, the Whitneys would have rid themselves of an unwelcome kinsman and closed the mouth of one who might be a policeman.

Jeff licked dry lips. He had never killed a man and knew that he could never kill. He tried to think of some way out, of something he could do, and there was nothing. Jeff licked his lips again.

"What say you?" Barr demanded. "It-it's a crazy idea!"

"'Tis what ye wanted, what ye told the boy you'd git."

"I didn't tell him I'd get it this way. For heaven's sake, man, listen to reason! The law, and not me, should take care of this."

Barr's eyes flamed. "Are ye a policeman?" "No!"

"The boy said different."

"Mebbe," Grant said slowly, "'twould be best to shoot him. I'll go on Trilley Ridge with-with who used to be my kin."

Jeff heaved a great sigh. First things first, always a new customer down the road, and if he went on the ridge, he would have time to think. If he did not, his hours were numbered anyway. He said slowly, "Let it be your way, Barr."

Barr said quietly, "'Tis well ye say so, for 'twould not be right should a Whitney shoot a Whitney or be shot by one. D'ye lack aught?"

"My pack."

Barr looked curiously at him but Jeff made no attempt to satisfy his curiosity. He'd always been able to pull almost anything he needed out of his

pack and there should be something to help him now. He couldn't think of what it was, but the pack had been a part of him for so long that he would feel better if he had it.

"Whar's the pack?" Barr asked. "At Granny Wilson's."

"Get it an' fetch it," Barr directed Yancey. "D'ye need aught else?" Jeff's brain was still whirling. "No."

Barr glanced inquiringly at Pete, who stared like a vicious animal and said nothing. There was finality in Barr's words. "Ask no more for it shall not be given. Both have had your say."

The words hammered dully at Jeff's ears. Then he awoke with a start and swallowed twice. For the first time he became aware of the shotgun shells that weighted his pocket. They were even more harmless than so many stones, for they were still loaded with paper.

But he'd been given a chance to speak and he had not spoken.

Pal went wild with joy when Jeff returned from Ackerton. He stayed as close as he could get, for he had missed his master greatly and needed him sorely. He smirked at the white kitten when he spotted it, but made no hostile move because Jeff had brought it. Wholly contented, Pal lay at Jeff's feet while he breakfasted and talked with Granny and Dan.

When Jeff rose to leave, Pal danced happily to the door and wagged his tail in anticipation. Everything was once more as it had been and should be. They were about to go peddling together on the trails. The big dog glanced back to see if Dan was coming, too. Instead, the boy grasped his collar.

"You stay here."

Pal flattened his ears and drooped his tail. But he was not allowed to go. For a full minute he stood hopefully in front of the door. Then he went sadly back into the kitchen.

Playing with a ball of paper that Granny had wadded up and thrown on the floor, the fluffy kitten arched its back and spat. Pal paid no attention. His heart was heavy and joy had gone with Jeff.

All the rest of the morning he was a wooden dog who did not even rouse himself when Yancey Whitney came to the door, said that Jeff wanted his pack, and went away with it. That afternoon he followed Dan about the hill, but he had no eyes for the sheep, the cow, the mule, and he lacked zest even for chasing blackbirds that came to pillage Granny's garden. He cared only about the trail up which Jeff had come and down which he had gone again.

That night, after Dan and Granny had gone to bed, Pal padded restlessly over to the door. Eagerly he sniffed every wind that blew and every scent that tickled his nose. He knew when six deer, feeling safe in the cover of night, came out of the forest and climbed the hill to graze in the sheep pasture. He heard a mouse rustle, and he was aware when a night-flying owl cruised

past the door. All these things he smelled or heard. He felt only the absence of his master.

The night was very deep and very black when Pal's yearning for Jeff became unbearable. He pushed his nose against the door, and when he did so the latch rattled slightly. He pricked up his ears and bent his head toward the noise, but he did not understand any of the mysterious ways by which people fastened things.

Softly he reared against the door, sniffing at every crack. Getting down, he trembled anxiously. Then, inch by inch, he began a second inspection of the door.

It was completely accidental when, in raising his head, he pushed the latch upward and the door swung open. Pal did not linger to think about anything else; he knew only that the way was clear. He flew into the night, found Jeff's trail and raced along it.

At Johnny Blazer's cabin, he scented Jeff's trail and that of five Whitneys-the pack-laden Yancey had gone back there-leading into the hills. Pal followed along.

He halted momentarily at the foot of Trilley Ridge, for Dabb Whitney was sitting on a big rock and the smell of his pipe was rank and heavy in the darkness. Pal slipped past, knowing that he could not be seen in the night. He caught the odor of wood smoke. Then, mingled with it, were the scents of Pete and Barr Whitney and of Jeff. Abandoning the trail, Pal followed his nose to his beloved master.

He came to the cabin and scratched on the door.

12. SURPRISE

They came to the cabin on Trilley Ridge after dark, Jeff and Pete walking side by side and Barr silent behind them. Jeff balanced the pack on his shoulders and was glad he had it there. It was an old friend and had always been a true one. He had been in trouble many times while it was on his shoulders, but he had never stayed in trouble.

As they walked he tried to pinpoint directions, but because of the darkness he could not do so. They had left the road for a path so faint that the casual traveler would not even see it as he passed. There was another path, and still another, and all of it was country that the hill men knew well but that Jeff did not know at all. When they finally reached the cabin, he was sure only that it was north of the road. But it would not have been an unpleasant journey if Pete had not been walking with him.

Found out, Pete had retreated sullenly into himself and Jeff again thought of an animal. But Pete was no ordinary savage thing that might attack because it was hungry or seeking a fight. He planned, and hidden behind his weak blue eyes was a crafty brain. Jeff knew that Pete's only thought revolved around ways to kill him, and it was a cold thing to know.

The men came to the cabin and Barr said, "This is hit."

Jeff spoke over his shoulder. "You sure the place isn't haunted?"

"No ha'nts." Barr seemed perplexed, as though there was something about the mission he no longer understood. "Push the door an' go in."

"Sure," Jeff said agreeably.

He opened the door and felt Pete go tense beside him. Jeff gripped his shotgun with both hands, preparing to bring it crashing down on the man's head. Pete would kill without imperiling himself, if he could, and almost his only chance would occur when they entered the dark cabin. But Barr knew this too.

"Stay here," he ordered his cousin. And to Jeff, "Got a match in your pocket?"

"Yep."

"Go in by yourself an' light hit. Strike hit to the tallow candle that'll be settin' on the table."

Jeff entered, felt the cabin's walls enclose him, and had a strange feeling that Barr Whitney was a complete fool. It would be simple to swing suddenly, cock the

88

shotgun as he swung and, always supposing he had some live ammunition, send a leaden hail back through the door. Then he understood.

Barr was no fool. He had merely gauged Jeff and he knew men. He had known that Pete would turn and shoot if sent in first, but Jeff would not. Besides, Jeff thought wryly, though Pete might be forced to stand in any line of fire that might sweep out the door, Barr would be elsewhere.

Jeff took a match from his pocket, struck it, and looked around the cabin. It was one fairly large room, and at the far end was a natural stone fireplace. There was a table, three chairs, two double bunks built one on top of the other, cooking utensils hanging from wooden pegs driven into the wall, and small windows. The cabin was either a bachelor's home or else it was used only on occasion by some person or persons who had reason to spend time here. Jeff touched his dying match to the fat tallow candle that stood on the table and flicked the burned match onto the floor.

"Come on in," he said cheerfully. "And welcome to our happy home!"

Pete's face was cold, and that was almost the only expression. He strode to a chair, pulled it away from the table and sat down with his rifle across his lap. Jeff stood his shotgun in a corner and turned to face Barr.

"Snug little den," he said pleasantly.

Barr looked puzzled and said nothing. However, the burning determination and the sternness were partly gone from his face. This was a serious business but Jeff was not accepting it seriously. Never flicking his eyes from his captives, Barr pulled a chair very close to the door.

"Here we be," he pronounced, "an' here we stay 'til the sun lightens the topmost twigs on the big pines."

"That's cute," Jeff declared admiringly. "That's really cute!" Barr glared at him. "What is?"

"Your description. "Til the sun lightens the topmost twigs on the big pines.' Not exactly poetry, but it has a poetic spirit. Well, if we're going to be here all night, we should do something besides glare at each other."

He slid out of the pack, laid it on the table and stretched. Then he stifled a yawn. He'd had no sleep last night and evidently he'd get none tonight, but more than once he'd had to stay awake as long, and he could do it again.

"If you be weary," Barr indicated the bunks, "you might sleep." "Thanks," Jeff declined, "but I'm afraid I'd have bad dreams. Besides,

this may be my last chance to talk with you. What'll we talk about, Barr?" Barr broke out suddenly, "I can't plumb ya. Can't plumb ya a'tall!"

Jeff said smoothly, "It's easy. I'm not a complex person. I'll tell you my life story if you want to hear it. Won't cost you a cent."

"I swan!" Barr ejaculated. "I could like ye a lot if'n I didn't-"

"If you didn't think I was a policeman? Sorry I can't change your mind on that subject. But I'm not."

Barr's eyes searched Jeff's. "Why'd the boy say it?"

I am."

Jeff shrugged. "If I knew why boys say things, I'd be a lot smarter than

89

"But ya did tell the boy ya'd find out who kil't Blazer?" "Yup."

"Yet, now ye got the chanst, you'd pass it by?"

"This is a chance? I don't want to kill anybody. I never promised Dan anything except that we'd find his father's murderer. Afterwards I was going to turn him over to the law."

Barr wrinkled his brows. "But ye be no policeman?"

"I'm not," Jeff said flatly. "Barr, what had you intended to do with me?" It was Barr's turn to shrug. "Shoot ya."

"And in your opinion, that was right?"

Barr said fiercely, "A body don't stop to think should he tromp on its haid does he find a pizen snake on his h'arthstone!"

Jeff lapsed into silence. His life story he had offered in jest, but he understood Barr's. His ancestors had been among the first to come to America, and they had come because there wasn't room enough for them in Europe. But neither had there been room enough in America's scattered colonies for people so fierce, reckless and proud. They had either left the settlements of their own accord or been driven out. They had wanted above all to live by their own personal inclinations and not by rules which they had little part in making. Always they had sought the wildest and most inaccessible places because only there could they live as they must.

Barr Whitney typified this wild independence, which couldn't possibly endure. Sooner or later even the hill clans must submit to the forward march of civilization and Jeff hoped that the advancing juggernaut would not crush them completely. The spirit they represented always had been and always would be necessary to free people. Probably the older ones would go down fighting; certainly they would never learn that they must bend themselves to others. Perhaps their children, or their children's children, would.

Jeff shrugged. That was to come. This was now, and neither civilization nor anything else had as yet tamed Barr Whitney. Jeff rubbed a hand on his trousers.

"You ail?" Barr asked. "My hand's twitching."

"The oil of shunk an' the grease of b'ar, mixed two of one to one of the other, an' cooked on a hick'ry fire when the moon's near horn points to water, will drive out ary itch."

Jeff grinned. "Can't wait for the moon's near horn to point to water, and besides I don't want a cure. When my hand twitches, I'm lucky."

Pete moved so swiftly that he seemed in one split second to be sitting on his chair and then, magically, to be standing with his rifle at half raise. But

quick as he was, Barr was quicker. His rifle cracked, a lock of hair detached itself from Pete's head to float softly to the floor, and before the sound died Barr had levered another cartridge into the chamber. He spoke as casually as though he had just shot at a squirrel.

"Next'un's goin' through your haid, Pete. Si' down."

Pete sat. Barr grinned. Jeff dared let himself think of the prospect that awaited.

Tomorrow morning, side by side and at exactly the same time, Jeff and

Pete would be allowed to leave the cabin. Jeff pulled his stomach in, as though he could already feel Pete's slug ripping through it. Again he pondered escaping, but all he could think of was what he had already considered.

If he ran, one of the waiting Whitneys would shoot him down when he came off the ridge. There was little chance of doing anything tonight; Barr was along to see that he didn't. He couldn't protect himself with paper bullets. Jeff had a wild notion of whirling as they stepped out the door, smashing Pete over the head with the muzzle of his shotgun, and trying to claim him as prisoner. But that was a very wild plan which had almost no chance of success. Pete was far too quick and far too expert a rifleman.

Jeff put such thoughts behind him. No man could do anything well if he tried to do more than one thing at a time, and first things must be first. He shivered.

"How about a fire, Barr?"

"Lay a blaze if'n ye want. Thar's wood in the box."

Jeff laid a fire, lighted it and stood with his back to the fireplace as flames crackled. He looked at a darkened window and had a curious thought that this night would never end. It should, he decided, have passed long ago. But when he looked at his watch, it was only half past nine.

He should be hungry but he wasn't. They'd eaten in Johnny Blazer's cabin, and now he was too nervous to eat. After a very long interval, he looked again at his watch.

It was a quarter to ten.

Jeff glanced at his pack and created mental images of the goods it contained. There were knives, fishing tackle, a half dozen new mouth organs, fiddle strings, gay ribbons, scissors, needles-He had bought only what the hill people wanted, and among all of it he could not think of a single article that would help him now.

Jeff set his jaw. Maybe, if there was something to do, time would not drag so slowly and, besides, he could think better when he was busy. "Play cards?" he invited.

"No." Barr shook his head. "Oh, come on!"

Barr tipped his head toward Pete, who sat motionless, with his rifle across his lap. Unmoving, he missed nothing and was ready at a split second notice to take advantage of anything that offered.

"Take his rifle away," Jeff urged. "You can still watch him." "A body has the right to keep his rifle."

"He sure is nursing it." Jeff felt reckless. "How about sitting in, Pete?

We don't have to shoot each other before morning."

Pete refused to answer. Jeff pulled his chair to the table and tried to entertain himself with solitaire. But he was too tense and strained to concentrate, and when he found himself adding the four of hearts to the seven of spades, he shoved the cards across the table and let them lay there. Restlessly he threw another chunk of wood on the fire and turned to Barr.

With no noise, and almost without effort, Barr rose. His eyes were alert and his face was intent. He backed, so that while continuing to command the cabin and the

91

two in it, he could control the door, too. There was a rasping scratch on the door and Barr said softly, "See what's thar. See who's a'visitin'."

Jeff opened the door and Pal panted in. His ears were flat and his tail hang-dog as, giving Barr a wide berth and glancing suspiciously at Pete, he went to the far end of the cabin and stood. Not knowing whether or not he was to be punished for leaving Granny's, he looked expectantly at his master. Jeff laughed and twitched his fingers.

"Come here, you old flea cage."

Grinning happily, Pal came at once and Jeff brushed his shaggy head with an affectionate hand. He was less tense and, strangely, his anxiety lessened. The great dog wagged an ecstatic tail while Jeff continued to pat his head.

For a short space, delighted to be near each other once more, neither had paid attention to anything else. Pal licked Jeff's face with a big, sloppy tongue and wagged everything from his muzzle to the tip of his tail. He turned to growl at Barr and Pete, and Barr flicked his rifle.

"I wouldn't leave him try it." "I won't," Jeff promised.

He slipped two fingers beneath Pal's collar, led him over to the table and sat down. Bending over Pal, as though continuing to caress him, he hoped Barr could not hear his pounding heart, and was glad his eyes were hidden. After a moment, Jeff raised his head.

He looked too casually at the candle that flickered a foot from his hand. Trying to appear disinterested, he gauged Pete's exact distance and Barr's position. He moistened dry lips with his tongue and reviewed his suddenly- formed plan.

Even though he risked a burned hand doing it, he was positive that he could snuff the candle out before Barr could shoot. Then he'd tip the table over

and fight his way out. Jeff nibbled his lower lip and looked doubtfully at Pal. Barr was supple as an eel and strong as an ox; Jeff might need help and could he count on Pal?

Barr asked suspiciously, "What ye flustered about?"

Jeff muttered silently at himself. He had a plan. If it was desperate, the situation called for desperate measures. But everything depended on surprise. To give Barr the slightest warning would also give him time to shoot Jeff. It went without saying that he would then be able to shoot Pal, and Jeff hadn't the least doubt that Barr would be happy to do both. He forced a laugh.

"It's just nice to see something around here that's not hell-bent to shoot something else."

Barr remained alert. "Whar'd ye get Blazer's dog?"

"Found him over beyond Cressman," Jeff said truthfully. "Do you keep dogs?"

"Houn's," Barr admitted. "Wouldn't pester myself with a no-account dog such as that."

Jeff cast for a way to lull Barr. "Depends on what you want in a dog, wouldn't you say?"

"Could. What do you want?"

Jeff did his best to look like a man who faces a desperate situation, but who was mightily cheered because his dog saw fit to track him down. If he did everything exactly right, and with split-second precision, his plan had at least an even chance of working.

Escape would not solve everything. Pete would still be unpunished and if the Whitneys should meet him, Jeff, again, they would not bother to take him prisoner. They'd shoot on sight. But he could name Johnny Blazer's killer. That would start things, and maybe he'd be able to finish them.

Regardless of what might happen in the future, this was now. Jeff had to get out of the cabin before he could do anything else, but it was as though Barr could read his mind.

"You're ponderin'," he accused. "Is that a crime in these hills?"

"If," Barr said deliberately, "you try to make a break, I'll kill ye in your tracks. I have spoke it."

Jeff said irritably, "Don't be a darn fool!"

"Don't you be one, nuther. You're gettin' a chanst."

"Yes," Jeff sighed, "a big chance." He looked again at the candle. "Any of your hounds ever get you out of jail, Barr?"

"Pah! How might a houn' do such?" "Well, Pal got me out."

"Those words I mistrust."

"He did," Jeff insisted. "It was in Cressman-"

He told of the Cressman jail and of how he was literally thrown out of it because, when he played the mouth organ, Pal howled. He spoke of inquiring the way to Delview as a ruse to throw Pop and Joe Parker from his trail, for he suspected that they had intended to have him rearrested there. Instead of going to Delview, he had come over the hills to Smithville.

Barr chuckled derisively. "Peddlin' teach you sech tall tales?" "It's true."

"Ha! You toot music an' the dog howls?" "Let me show you."

Jeff took a mouth organ from his pack, blew a soft note and Pal responded with a moaning wail that trailed out on a soft soprano note.

Barr seemed dumfounded. "Doggone!"

Jeff's eyes strayed to the candle. Barr rose, wrenched it from its drippings and put it down at the far end of the table. He resumed his seat. "I can see best when hit's thar," he announced grimly. "You wa'nt havin' notions 'bout that candle, was you?"

"Why, no, of course not."

Jeff managed to appear innocent, even while he mentally kicked himself. His chance had come and gone. There'd be another chance and Barr seemed more at ease.

"This night I learn't what I knew not. A dog howls to noise." "This one does."

"Make him do hit ag'in. 'Tis a mighty curious thing."

Jeff blew another note and Pal howled again. Barr's eyes sparkled. An elemental creature himself, he was interested in the elemental and this fascinated him. He must find the answer, but while seeking it he did not forget to keep his eyes on Jeff and Pete.

"Why's he do hit?" he asked.

"I don't know," Jeff admitted. "Can't figure it myself." "Have him do hit some

93

more."

At the first note, Pal obliged with a banshee wail that subsided, then gathered force and mounted again. The sound filled the cabin and offered the illusion of being not only real, but all reality. It was as though the door burst open of its own accord, and Jeff rubbed his eyes in disbelief.

Ike Wilson stood framed in the doorway.

He was slim, supple, smiling, but behind the smile there was something hard as stone and there was nothing to provoke humor in the cocked, double-barreled shotgun he carried. Half erect in his chair, Barr froze there. Pete's face turned white. Ike grinned happily.

"Hi, peddler!"

"Hi, Ike! Where the blazes did you come from?"

"Broadview Prison. Stopped by Granny's an' she told me you was about. Heerd the dog howl an' calc'lated you'd be nigh." His chuckle was rich and very audible. "I didn't expect a hul nest of you. Good thing I peered in the window glass afore I come in."

Barr snarled, "This ain't your mix!"

"Oh, yes, it is! Yes, it is my mix! Now just hand me that lil' old rifle gun, Barr. Stock foremost."

Fighting against so doing but unable to help himself, Barr relinquished his rifle. Ike threw it through the open door.

"Now, Pete," he coaxed, "I need your'n."

Pete remained rooted. Smiling, but with a deadly something behind the smile, Ike tightened his finger on the shotgun's trigger.

"Don't like to shoot settin' pat'tidges, but I will."

Pete handed his rifle over. Ike tossed it out and slammed the door. Holding the shotgun with one hand, he drew a length of buckskin from his pocket and whipped it straight. He spoke as though he were addressing a petulant child. "Now just put your hands behin't the chair, Barr. This shotgun might go off accidental like, an' it makes quite a hole."

Tight-lipped, Barr did as he was ordered. Expertly Ike laced his hands and then his feet. He approached Jeff apologetically.

"'Feard I'll have to tie you too, peddler." "But-"

"Now don't gimme no fuss." Ike rubbed the friendly Pal's head. "Jest do like Uncle Ike says."

Jeff thrust his hands behind the chair and permitted himself to be bound. Ike slipped a rawhide thong through Pal's collar and tied him to the chair rung. He stood erect and looked around, his manner that of one who has just done a job and done it well.

Jeff asked, "What's the big idea, Ike?"

Ike chuckled again. "Business! Say, how come these Whitneys had a gun on you?"

"Barr," Jeff inclined his head, "had the idea that I'm a policeman."

"Fer snort's sake!" Ike faced Barr. "Your brain soft? He's a peddler an' a good 'un.

I ought to know. I was in jail with him."

"Leave me loose," Barr snarled, "an' I won't hurt ye." "'Pears to me you won't anyhow."

"Ye'll not git back down the ridge!"

"Now, now," Ike soothed, "jest leave that to Uncle Ike. I got up it, didn't I?"

Ike whirled to face Pete and something inside of Jeff turned cold. He had seen angry men, but suddenly he knew that not even Barr Whitney was as strong in anger as Ike Wilson. It was an inward quality, for outwardly he remained very gentle and he did not raise his voice.

"I come fer Bucky."

Pete muttered sullenly, "Got nothin' to do with Bucky."

"Oh, yes, you have," Ike corrected him. "Yes, you have. Bucky's still in Broadview, but you're goin' to help get him out. Bet that if you strained yourself, you could mind the night we got Wheeler's chickens. You was goin' to stay behin't, you said, an' leave us know should somebody come. But when the police come, you was a long ways behin't. What'd they pay you fer turnin' us in, Pete?"

Sweat glistened on Pete's brow. "I had naught to do with it!"

"You'll never git anywhere, Pete, lyin' in such a way. Are you comin' like a little man, or am I goin' to scatter your spare parts from here to Cressman?"

Pete gasped, "What you goin' to do with me?"

"Jest lay in the hills," Ike soothed. "Leastwise we'll lay thar 'til I can send word to that smart Joe Parker. Goin' to tell him, I am, that I know who stuck up the Cressman bank. Goin' to tell him that, when Bucky comes into the hills, he'll find that man tied to a tree. I reckon Parker'll swap for that."

"If he doesn't," Jeff said suddenly, "you can offer more. Pete killed Johnny Blazer!"

"He did?" Ike's eyes glowed eagerly. "Now I know I got me a swap!

Come 'long, Pete."

Herding his captive, he started for the door. Suddenly he stopped and ordered, "Wait thar!"

Pete stood still. Ike glided to Jeff, sliced the bonds that tied his hands, and bent to whisper, "Gimme five minutes, peddler-jest five minutes an' kiss Granny fer me."

"I will," Jeff promised, "and I'll tell her that you'll deliver one to her yourself in a few days."

He waited ten minutes before stooping to untie his feet. He rose, and before freeing Barr he glanced out of one of the small windows.

The first hint of dawn was in the sky and the horizon was endless. He had found binding ties in these hills, but somehow he had found limitless freedom, too.

THE END

95

JIM KJELGAARD was born in New York City. Happily enough, he was still in the pre- school age when his father decided to move the family to the Pennsylvania mountains. There young Jim grew up among some of the best hunting and fishing in the United States. He says: "If I had pursued my scholastic duties as diligently as I did deer, trout, grouse, squirrels, etc., I might have had better report cards!"

Jim Kjelgaard has worked at various jobs-trapper, teamster, guide, surveyor, factory worker and laborer. When he was in the late twenties he decided to become a full-time writer. He has published several hundred short stories and articles and quite a few books for young people.

His hobbies are hunting, fishing, dogs, and questing for new stories. He tells us: "Story hunts have led me from the Atlantic to the Pacific and from the Arctic Circle to Mexico City. Stories, like gold, are where you find them. You may discover one three thousand miles from home or, as in THE SPELL OF THE WHITE STURGEON, right on your own door step." And he adds: "I am married to a very beautiful girl and have a teen-age daughter. Both of them order me around in a shameful fashion, but I can still boss the dog! We live in Phoenix, Arizona."

www.ingramcontent.com/pod-product-compliance
Lightning Source LLC
Chambersburg PA
CBHW020632130626
46552CB00003B/1192